"Fast paced and full of action."   —*ForeWord Magazine*

"I was captivated by *Captured*. I found the second book in this great series as entertaining and action filled as the first book."   —TCM Reviews

"An intense storyline that will have you churning through the book without putting it down."   —The Super Mom

"I would give this book three thumbs up, but I only have two thumbs."   —7th grade student, MSTA Newsletter

"A sequel that matches the pace and excitement of the original. In *Captured*, the author has added a second gem to the reading treasure chest."   —The Reading Tub

"A delightful tale of kids working together, much as you would find in the *Lemony Snicket* books. Readers will look forward to more."

—Curled Up With a Good Kids Book

"Will keep you on the edge of your seat while begging you to read on . . . full of fast paced action (that) keeps the reader wanting more. I eagerly await the third book."

—Steve Fielman, Director-at-large,
Intermediate Science, New York State

"Holds even an adult readers attention to the very end. I look forward to his next offering in the series."

—AAAS

"With *Captured,* the author continues to tell a story that leaves the reader reaching for chapter after chapter with plenty of suspense and cliff hangers. This is a fun and adventurous story."

—California Science Teachers Association

Praise for
THE PROMETHEUS PROJECT: TRAPPED

"A thriller that you won't put down until you've reached the last page."   —Kids' Picks, *Odyssey Magazine*

"*Trapped* is a complete thrill ride."   —TCM Reviews

"This adventure will keep kids turning the pages . . . perfect for middle grades." —*Teaching Pre K-8 Magazine*

"Highly recommended for both boys and girls. Wonderful and unique."   —Discovery Journey

"My class loved it. They were totally engaged. It's a hard book to put down."
                              —Jeff Montag, 5th Grade Teacher
                    As Quoted in the *San Diego Union-Tribune*

"Cinematic. Readers will surely be reminded of Eleanor Cameron's *Mushroom Planet* series, as well as Heinlein's *Have Space Suit—Will Travel,* and even Clarke's *2001.* Vividly speculative. Able to capture the imagination of any teen."   —*Asimov's Science Fiction* magazine

"Keeps you turning the pages. It had me hooked by page two of the first book."   —The Children's Book Review

"Captures that pulse-pounding excitement you remember from your *Have Spaceship Will Travel* and *Postmarked the Stars* days. Crisp, clean, and delivers what it promises."
                                                    —SFReader.com

"Brings to mind the classic young reader's novel A *Wrinkle in Time.* An adventure story for young and old alike."
                                                    —Associated Content

"Fun and suspenseful. Highly recommended."
                                                    —*Kirkus Discoveries*

"An entertaining novel . . . that reads in a flash."
—Bookloons Reviews

"The gripping storyline will make young readers read this story in one sitting and want a sequel. I strongly recommend this book." —The Midwest Book Review

"I did not want to stop reading."
—8th Grade Student
Published in the Newsletter of the ISTA

"If you have a middle schooler that is into science or sci-fi, buy this book. If you have a reluctant reader who has an interest in science or adventure stories, buy this book."
—Amateur de Livre Book Reviews

"I read this book with my class for the first time this year and my class loved it."
—President, Idaho Science Teachers Association

"Brilliant. Perfect for a class reader for 9-13s, and a 'must' for any school library. These books are, I hope, the first of a long series!" —*Primary Science* (UK Journal)

"Nonstop action adventure . . . You really can't put the book down for very long. A thrilling read."
—California Science Teachers Association

The Prometheus Project

Book 2

Captured

The Prometheus Project

Book 2
Captured

Douglas E. Richards

Paragon Press

Paragon Press Edition copyright © 2010
Second Edition published by Paragon Press, 2010
ParagonPressSF@gmail.com

ISBN: 978-0-9826184-2-4

Library of Congress Control Number: 2009944189

Printed in the United States of America

First Paragon Edition

Contents

Contents

The Prometheus Project

Book 2

Captured

PROLOGUE

Trapped

Ryan and Regan Resnick were sure their lives had been ruined forever. Without any warning their parents, both leading scientists, had announced they would be moving from San Diego to a house in the middle of the Pennsylvania woods. They were forced to leave their friends to move to a town so small that most of its roads weren't even paved. How could this happen to them? They were sure they would soon die of boredom.

They would soon be in danger of dying, all right—but definitely not from boredom. In fact, they didn't know it at the time, but they were just days away from the greatest adventure of their lives.

It had all begun when they were looking for something stored in a box in their attic just after the move. This is when they overheard their parents' strange and suspicious conversation about a place, and a project, called Prometheus. When they investigated further, their lives had changed forever.

Soon they were hopping razor-wire fences, solving security passwords and tricking guards to discover a vast underground city, built by a super-advanced alien race for unknown purposes. They learned that their parents were members of the Prometheus Project, an ultra-top-secret team of top scientists and elite security guards assembled by the president to explore the fantastic, abandoned city.

The city was surrounded by a thin force-field, an energy barrier that was impossible to penetrate—or even to scratch. Only the genius of their father, Ben Resnick, enabled the team to finally break through the barrier and into the amazing city. And what they found inside was truly astonishing. The level of technology the alien builders had used was not only far beyond human ability, but beyond human understanding.

While the force-field deep underground that surrounded the city was shaped like a hollow hockey-puck—about one mile around and thirty feet high—the city was many, many times larger than this, and its ceiling was so high it couldn't be seen with the naked eye. How could anything be far larger on the inside than it was on the outside? How could something buried in a confined space underground have a seemingly endless blue sky? The city could well have been located outdoors, judging by appearances, if not for the eerie fact that the sun could never be found within its bright, cloudless sky. The existence of such a city was completely impossible, of course, but it was clear that the aliens hadn't let that stop them from building it.

The astonishing size of the buried city was just one of its mysteries. Inside the alien city the team immediately found many more. Fantastic structures of every kind. Buildings that could morph from one form to another. A walkway made of spongy material that would trampoline users forward, and always in such a way that they maintained perfect balance. A staircase made from almost invisible threads that were far stronger than steel. And all this had been discovered in a single day! The treasure trove of advanced technology that awaited the human explorers was truly endless.

But the team knew they had to be careful. Very careful. They had chosen the name Prometheus so they would always be reminded of this. Prometheus was a Titan of Greek mythology who had stolen fire from the Gods and given it to humankind as a gift. Like fire, the city's technology had the power to change human civilization forever, but also like fire, it could be unbelievably dangerous.

After discovering the city and learning of the Prometheus Project, Ryan and Regan had pleaded with the team's leader, Dr. Harry Harris, to let them become part of the team. While he had been very impressed with the talent they had shown by overcoming extensive security measures to discover and enter the alien city, he had refused. They were just kids, after all.

They were about to be escorted out of the city, forever, when a heavy generator had fallen and severely injured their mom. The kids ran for help. When they returned, just a minute later, the entire team had disappeared! They had vanished, without any evidence that they had even existed. Worse still, Ryan and Regan soon learned the entrance to the city was gone as well. They were trapped! Trapped and alone inside a dangerous, alien city.

What had happened to the team? What had happened to the entrance? And how long would it be before the same thing happened to them?

Before their adventure was over, they were able to find the answers to all of these questions—and more. They discovered a zoo building that allowed them to visit other planets instantly. They forged a friendship with a telepathic computer called the Teacher. They learned who had built the city and why. Finally, they figured out exactly what had happened to their parents and the others and were able to save their mother's life.

Just another boring day in Pennsylvania.

Dr. Harris was impressed. Very impressed. They had made enormous contributions to the team. Their courage and capabilities were truly remarkable. After all they had done, Dr. Harris changed his mind and agreed to let them become members of the team. They had certainly earned it.

Their discovery of the alien city and these adventures are all chronicled in the book, *The Prometheus Project: Trapped*. The Resnick kids were certain that nothing they would ever do the rest of their lives could possibly be more exciting, or more important.

They were wrong.

Six months had now passed since the events in *The Prometheus Project: Trapped*. During this time, when Ryan and Regan weren't attending school, they spent almost every waking minute in the alien city, helping the scientists explore the most important discovery in the history of the world. Life could not have been more exciting. And so far, they had not encountered any further dangers.

But this was about to change.

They had no way of knowing it, but they were about to embark on yet another adventure—one even more demanding and more dangerous than their first.

And this time, there would be more—far more—than just their lives, and the lives of the Prometheus team, hanging in the balance.

CHAPTER 1

A Warning

"Yessss!" said Ryan Resnick happily, pumping his fist in the air. *Finally.* The three o'clock bell had rung. The *Friday* bell. The weekend had officially arrived.

Ryan bolted out of the classroom, down the stairs, and outside to his bike securely padlocked to one of the school's many bike-racks. He was so eager to take off he thought he might actually jump out of his skin. But after three full minutes there was still no sign of his sister Regan, two years younger than him.

"Regan," he thought as hard as he could, straining to broadcast the thought as forcefully as possible. *"Where are you?"*

"Sorry," came the telepathic response. *"Held up by a teacher. Be right there."*

A few seconds later Regan shot through the door.

8

She had strawberry blond hair, a freckled face, and green eyes that always seemed to sparkle.

"Let's get going," said Ryan impatiently as he saw her and then, realizing this wasn't a very friendly greeting, added, "how was school?"

Regan quickly worked a combination lock and removed it from her bike. "Great," she replied as she stuffed the lock in a pouch attached to her handlebars. "Fantastic even." She paused, raised her eyebrows, and added, "Then again, when you've explored Prometheus, it's hard to get excited about school."

Ryan nodded as he and his sister jumped on their bikes and took off.

Their school really was terrific. No money had been spared on the facility, the teachers were excellent, and the students were eager to learn; many of them children of accomplished scientists. In the few months the new school had been open they had both made numerous friends. But nothing could *possibly* compare to Prometheus. Nothing on Earth, at any rate. One day they hadn't know about the astonishing alien city and the next it had become, by far, the most important part of their lives.

Not only had their first visit to the alien city forever changed the course of their lives, it had changed *them*— given them new abilities. This was almost certainly due to their interactions with the city's unbelievably advanced, telepathic central computer. Because they had first activated it inside an alien classroom it had introduced itself simply as the Teacher. The Teacher was wonderful and they had rapidly developed a very special relationship with it.

During their first telepathic conversation with the Teacher they had developed splitting headaches and it was forced to end the conversation in mid-sentence. The Teacher had realized that the telepathic frequency it was using was not compatible with their minds, and if it did not end the conversation it was in danger of damaging their brains. Later it was able to find a way to communicate with them telepathically without causing any damage, and even to temporarily speed up their brains so that it could have a lengthy conversation with them in less than a second. In this super-accelerated mode, their brains were working so quickly that even a speeding car would have appeared to them to be completely frozen in place, like a statue. In some way, something the Teacher had done during these interactions had subtly changed the structure of their minds.

Now, even though the Teacher wasn't really alive, they could always sense what they thought of as its *life-force,* a faint but comforting mental glow that told them it was still out there, still going about its business. And most astonishing of all, they had found that they were now telepathic! Well, at least with each other. And while it still required more effort to communicate telepathically than out loud, their skills continued to improve. Perhaps someday they would develop into full telepaths.

Their telepathy, and their adventures together, had brought them closer together than they ever would have believed. Since they had discovered Prometheus, working together and getting along had very quickly become as much a habit for them as arguing and teasing each other had been before.

They had been riding in the direction of the alien city for several minutes when Regan broke the silence. "So how was your day?" she asked.

"Great," said her brother. He had short, light brown hair, green eyes and a smile that made people feel comfortable around him. "We had a really cool discussion about pain in Mrs. Rosen's science class."

"Pain?" said Regan, confused. "What do you mean? Like how to cause it?"

Ryan rolled his eyes. "Yeah. Sure Regan. She was teaching us how to torture people."

Regan smiled, feeling a bit foolish. "Okay, maybe not how to cause it. How about how to get rid of it?"

"Nope." Ryan shook his head.

"Okay, I give up. What did you talk about?"

"Believe it or not, why it's important?"

"Why it's important?" she repeated in disbelief.

"You know. Why it exists in the first place."

"That's an easy one," said Regan confidently. "To make people miserable."

"So you think it would be better if there was no such thing as pain?"

11

She nodded. "It'd be great."

"I thought the same thing," admitted Ryan. "But think about this: what if you couldn't feel any pain and you put your hand on a hot burner without realizing it?"

After thinking about this for a few seconds, Regan could see where her brother was headed and her green eyes sparkled in delight. If you could feel pain, no distraction in the world could prevent you from instantly snatching your hand away from the burner. But if you couldn't, you might just leave it there, with horrible consequences.

"Cool," she said. "It's a warning system."

"Yeah. It's obvious when you think about it," said Ryan. "But I never did before. Pain lets you know when you're doing something harmful to yourself and also if you're damaged inside—in a way that's impossible to ignore. Suppose you were a quarterback and you fractured your throwing arm. Without pain you'd never know it. You'd keep throwing, which would just make the injury worse. But if you *could* feel pain, you'd be screaming and checking yourself into a hospital for an X-ray."

"I thought quarterbacks were supposed to be tough," said Regan, grinning. "Do they really scream when they fracture their arms?"

Ryan laughed. "That's a good question. I don't know. I've never actually been close enough to a quarterback who was fracturing his arm to tell."

"We may never know," quipped Regan. "It probably isn't easy finding a quarterback willing to do that experiment."

Ryan smiled.

"Okay," continued Regan on a more serious note. "But once pain warns you that you're hurt, it sure would be nice if you could just turn it off."

"We talked about that, too," said Ryan. "It turns out—"

A thunderous burst of telepathy exploded into their minds!

Ryan instantly forgot what he was saying and he and his sister barely managed to keep their bikes from crashing.

"WARNING. UNAUTHORIZED ENTRY. WARNING. UNAUTHORIZED ENTRY. WARNING. UNAUTHOR—"

Just like that, the immensely powerful telepathic message stopped, as abruptly as it had begun.

And at the same time, the faint glow in their minds that represented the reassuring presence of the Teacher, the city's extraordinary computer, vanished, leaving nothing but a cold, unsettling emptiness in its place.

CHAPTER 2

A Possible Intruder

Regan stopped her bike abruptly and realized that Ryan had done the same.

"What just happened?" she said worriedly.

Ryan shook his head. "I don't know, but I'm pretty sure it's bad. Can you still feel the Teacher?"

"No."

"I can't either. Do you think it's dead?"

Regan considered. It wasn't clear if it was ever alive, but she knew what he meant. "Maybe. But I doubt it. It's just too advanced for that. Maybe it needed to leave the city for a while. Maybe it doesn't want us to be aware of it anymore for some reason. It's hard to say."

Ryan nodded unhappily. "What do you make of the 'Unauthorized Entry' warning?"

Regan shrugged. "I don't know. But I'm pretty sure

it came from the city. And whoever sent it really wanted to make sure a telepath would get it. I didn't know telepathy could be so loud."

"Me neither," he said, wincing. "I wonder what caused it. Did someone from the Prometheus team go somewhere they weren't supposed to? Enter a structure they weren't supposed to?"

Regan thought about this. When they were in contact with the Teacher, it had told them the city was built by a race called the Qwervy. The Qwervy had dropped off a single tiny robot—a nano-robot—on Earth, and the nano-robot was programmed to make other nano-robots, and so on, until there were trillions of them: enough to build an enormous, elaborate underground city. Once the city was built, the nano-robots, or *nanobots* for short, served as the repair crew. Although harmless, they looked like a swarm of voracious insects as they went about rebuilding anything that needed repair.

The Qwervy used the city as a secret observation post. Using one of the many portals that connected the city to other worlds, they would check in on humanity every hundred years or so, trying to determine when humanity was mature enough to join the galactic community of advanced civilizations. Once Earth became a member, visitors could come at any time. Until then, however, only authorized Qwervy and a small number of others were permitted to come to Earth.

But the Qwervy's secret observation post was no longer secret. Humans had managed to find the city and break into it, something they shouldn't have been able to do for a long, long time and something that had surprised even the Qwervy. Their father, Ben Resnick, in fact, had been the man who had calculated how to break through the city's force-field barrier.

The Qwervy thought humanity was a promising species but also had a dark and dangerous side it needed to master. They had decided to let the trespassers remain in the city to see if the humans could learn from the city's technology rather than destroy themselves with it.

"I don't think anyone on the team caused it," said Regan finally. "The Teacher gave us full permission to explore the city. If there was something inside that was totally off-limits, it would've told us. Besides," she added, "it can use technology we can only dream of. If someone from the Prometheus team wanted to go somewhere the Teacher didn't want them to go, it could easily stop them."

"So what's going on? If the warning wasn't caused by anything the Prometheus team did, then it had to be caused by someone, or some . . . thing," he said worriedly, "entering the city through a portal."

"Maybe," said Regan, unconvinced. "But maybe not. Exactly when did the Teacher disappear, before or after the warning?"

Ryan stared off into space, a confused look on his face. "I'm not sure," he said finally. "The warning was so loud in my brain that I wasn't paying attention to whether the Teacher was still there or not. After it ended, I realized the Teacher was gone, but it might have gone just *before* the warning rather than just after. I don't know."

Regan thought about it for a few seconds and then shrugged her shoulders. "I'm not sure either," she admitted. "But I can't believe anything unauthorized could make it through a portal with the Teacher still here. Maybe the Teacher decided to leave, or had to repair itself for some reason, or change its programming, or . . . something . . . and this caused a false alarm."

"Then why did the warning just suddenly stop like it did?"

Regan shrugged. "I don't know. Maybe whatever caused the false alarm fixed itself. Maybe, with the Teacher gone, a blade of grass from an alien planet blew through a portal before the automatic portal security system could take over."

Ryan considered. She could be right. It could just be a false alarm. The fire alarm had sounded at school several times over the years, and so far it had always been due to either a false alarm or a fire drill.

Ryan frowned. On the other hand, this didn't mean you could just ignore it. You always had to assume there really was a fire and leave the building. "I sure hope you're right," he said. "But we still need to check it out, just in case."

Regan nodded. "Okay," she said. "But exactly how are we going to do that?"

"Good question," replied Ryan. He shook his head in frustration. "I only wish I had a good answer for you."

CHAPTER 3

A Painful Assault

The Resnick siblings began riding toward the alien city once again.

"What about telling Dr. Harris and the team?" suggested Regan.

"What would we tell them?" said Ryan. "We can't tell them we can't feel the Teacher anymore, because they don't know about the Teacher. We can't tell them about the telepathic warning because they don't know we've become telepathic."

Regan frowned. He was right. The Qwervy had wanted to see how humanity handled the discovery of the city all on its own, so had instructed the Teacher to cease all communication with them and not to help humanity in any way. The Teacher had asked them to promise to keep its existence a secret and they had agreed. Since their telepathy stemmed from their inter-

19

actions with the Teacher they had decided not to tell anyone about this either.

They hated having to keep secrets from their parents and the team, but they had made a promise to the Teacher and it was one they intended to keep. After a few minutes of further discussion, however, they agreed on a strategy they thought would allow them to determine if the telepathic warning was a false alarm or not.

They reached the main Proact gate and were quickly waved through by the guards. Proact was a company that served as cover for the scientists on the Prometheus team, but also employed top scientists from every field who knew nothing about Prometheus. These scientists worked on advanced projects using *human* science and technology. The vast Proact grounds were enclosed by a razor-wire fence and protected by laser alarms and roving guards. The only access to the alien city, far underground—an enormous elevator housed inside a concrete bunker—was within this perimeter, but was protected far more extensively.

Once inside Proact, they passed though several additional checkpoints, provided several passwords, and had their fingerprints and retinas scanned electronically, a ritual they had come to know well. Finally, after ten minutes, they were at the last phase of their journey, inside the enormous Prometheus elevator as it plummeting downward toward the alien city.

Regan looked up toward the multiple cameras she knew

were hidden inside the elevator's ceiling and waved happily at the elevator guards who were monitoring their arrival down below. The kids were a favorite of the members of Prometheus security, and Regan knew that whoever was on elevator duty would appreciate any break from what was clearly the most boring security rotation of them all.

At last the elevator stopped and they stepped off into a massive, man-made cavern, the size of a baseball stadium, illuminated by powerful electric lights and filled with machinery and high-tech equipment.

They immediately recognized the two heavily armed guards who faced them as they exited the elevator, Captain Dan Walpus and Lieutenant Duncan Martin. Both were tall, clean-cut and athletic.

All of the members of Prometheus security were hand-picked by Colonel Carl Sharp, the head of security who had quickly become among their closest friends on the team. Colonel Sharp knew that he and his security team were absolutely necessary for a project of this importance, but he also didn't want the scientists to feel as though they had suddenly joined the military. To ensure they would be as comfortable around his men as possible, he insisted that his team wear civilian clothing and that everyone, including the two youngest members of the team, call them by their first names instead of their military titles.

Both men smiled warmly. "Hello kids," said Dan cheerfully. "How was school?"

"Great," they both said at once. "How are you guys doing?" added Regan.

Duncan shrugged. "You know. Same old, same old. The elevator goes up, the elevator comes down. The elevator goes up, the elevator comes down. So far, no bad guys."

"Fantastic," said Regan grinning. "Good work. I bet the place would be crawling with bad guys if it weren't for you."

"Absolutely," agreed Dan playfully.

"You know, that reminds me of a joke," said Regan. She paused for a moment to make sure she had it straight in her head. "A girl living in Pennsylvania sees a man dressed from head to toe in bright purple polka-dots," she began. "The girl asks the man why he is dressed like that. The man says, 'I'm dressed like this to scare off all the Kangaroos.' The girl raises her eyebrows and says, 'Kangaroos? But there *aren't any* Kangaroos in Pennsylvania!' To which the man replies, 'Exactly! You see how well it's working.'"

Both guards grinned from ear to ear. "Have we ever told you you're our favorite young woman on the team?" said Dan.

"You have," said Regan, her eyes twinkling. "And I keep telling you I'm the *only* young woman on the team."

"That doesn't make it any less true," countered Dan lightheartedly.

Ryan shook his head. He had witnessed similar exchanges all of his life. Regan had a playful, friendly personality that was infectious. He had never known anyone who could just naturally charm people the way his sister could. But as much as he didn't want to break up the fun, they were running a bit late and he was anxious to enter the alien city.

"Do you know if Carl is here today?" he asked Dan.

Dan nodded. "He's inside Prometheus. He should be there until late tonight."

"Thanks," said Ryan as he and Regan headed toward the far end of the cavern and the only entrance into the alien city.

They soon approached a familiar array of high-powered lasers, microwave force emitters, high-tech generators, and other advanced equipment unleashing a furious assault on the opaque force-field wall. Ben Resnick had figured out how to precisely tune this energy to counter-balance the frequency of the shield, inactivating, or nullifying, a large, rectangular section of it and creating an entrance to the city. This massive onslaught of energy had to be applied continuously to prevent the gap in the force-field from instantly closing.

As always, an ever-changing rainbow of colors danced across the opening, obscuring what was beyond. They calmly stepped through it and into Prometheus, a magnificent city sprawled out farther than the eye could see in every direction, including up. By some miracle of alien technology the city was immensely larger than the hole it had carved out deep in the earth of Pennsylvania.

A large row of top-of-the-line, electric-powered golf-carts were now parked beside the entrance: not only larger and faster than standard golf-carts, but far quieter as well. Beside these were parked a number of huge, electric trucks, all green, with rectangular cargo beds about three times the size of a standard pick-up. Four adults could fit comfortably in the vehicle's large front compartment, either sitting or standing. The team called these unique electric trucks "Haulers" because they were used to haul heavy scientific equipment around.

Both kids loved driving the golf-carts, but it was Ryan's turn, and he jumped into the driver's seat while his sister sat beside him. No matter how often they traveled within Prometheus the unusual and spectacular architecture and the exotic alien vegetation never got boring. They passed buildings that shimmered and others that changed colors depending on the angle from which they were viewed. Buildings that appeared to be floating and others that sparkled brilliantly as though made of diamonds. Some of the buildings were simple and elegant while others were in the shape of awe-inspiring geometric figures, like impossibly complex three-dimensional snowflakes that had come to life.

They had agreed to meet their parents at three-thirty and they were running a little late. Ryan quickly accelerated the cart to its top speed, and before too long the familiar zoo building he and his sister had discovered during their first adventure in the city came into view. As usual, amazingly real-looking holographic images of alien animals appeared one by one in front of the door, showing anyone passing what could be found inside.

Small though it was, the zoo building contained numerous doors, or portals, that each led to a different primitive planet. The Qwervy allowed visitors on these planets since none of them had intelligent life. Circular force-field barriers, similar to the Prometheus shield, completely surrounded the portal entrances on each planet to protect visitors from any dangerous animals, but a tram could be used to cross these force-field domes to explore.

Ryan passed the zoo—which was now showing the three-dimensional image of a giant creature, covered in red fur, with a body like a polar bear and a face like a crocodile—and stopped the cart in front of their parents' new laboratory building. It was octagonal, like a stop-sign, but silver instead of red. Their mother, Amanda Resnick, had specialized in predicting what alien life would be like, but she no longer had to predict: she was the first biologist on Earth who could actually study the real thing. She had set up shop in the building next door to the zoo and their father had set up his lab there as well.

The building appeared not to have any entrances, but appearances were deceiving. As the kids walked up to the middle of a solid wall a large panel seemed to dissolve, creating an entrance. Once they passed through it the wall rematerialized behind them. Regan had dubbed these "invisible doorways." While they were quite visible, it was impossible for anyone to know they were doorways just by looking at them, so the name was somehow appropriate.

Their parents were both wearing long white lab coats. Their father was sitting at a large, stainless-steel table in the center of the room studying a computer screen. Their mother, a short, attractive woman with soft features and blue eyes, was peering carefully through a powerful microscope at one end of the table.

The kids started to say hello. From out of nowhere their heads exploded in pain! Something was hammering at their brains and bringing pure agony in its wake.

They grabbed their ears as the merciless blast of searing pain hit them with such force they weren't even able to scream.

The pain was blinding, as if red-hot fireplace pokers were being jammed into each ear, stabbing relentlessly at their brains.

And there wasn't a doubt in either of their minds that if whatever was causing the pain didn't stop, they couldn't possibly survive it much longer.

CHAPTER 4

The Alien Device

R yan's legs felt rubbery and he knew he was nearing collapse.

"Ryan, leave the building. NOW!" came a shouted telepathic command from his sister, already outside of the building, which barely managed to find his conscious mind through the immense pain crushing his brain.

Somehow his legs obeyed her command and the next thing he knew he had joined his sister outside.

He gasped in relief as the pain ceased immediately. Regan was lying on the ground with an exhausted look on her face and he stumbled to the ground next to her. Although she had fled the building before sending her message, she wasn't in much better shape than he was.

An instant later their parents were kneeling over them wearing horrified expressions. They had looked up from their work just in time to read the agony on the faces of their children and then to see first Regan, and then Ryan, stagger out of the building.

"Are you okay?" asked Amanda Resnick worriedly. They both nodded.

"What happened?" asked their father.

Both kids told them about the sudden onset of overwhelming pain centered on their ears and head, and how it had dissipated immediately after they had exited the building.

"Great job, Regs," said Ryan warmly. "Thanks for saving me from that."

It never occurred to him that running from the building would help. He had assumed that whatever was happening to them would happen anywhere within the city.

Their parents looked confused. "I don't understand," said their father. "How did Regan help you?"

Ryan realized his mistake immediately. He had forgotten that his parents didn't hear his sister's telepathic shout.

"I don't know what he's talking about," said Regan, also realizing his mistake. "I *didn't* help him." Right after saying this she quickly broadcast, *"You're very welcome, Ryan. It's not like you haven't saved me before."*

All sets of eyes turned toward Ryan. "You know, now that I think about it," he said lamely, "she's right. I'm not sure what I meant just now."

Their parents exchanged worried looks. Ryan hallucinating help from his sister wasn't a good sign. Their mother examined them carefully and then had them answer a few simple math and science questions to be sure their memory and reasoning had not been affected.

Fortunately, after a few minutes they seemed to be doing well, and their parents were beginning to finally let out the mental breath they had been holding. Mrs. Resnick guessed that they would have been knocked unconscious in another ten or fifteen seconds had they stayed where they were. After that, who knew how long it would have been before they suffered permanent damage.

When their mother was absolutely convinced they had fully recovered, all four Resnicks made their way back to the large table at which Mr. and Mrs. Resnick had been seated when their children had arrived. They were understandably cautious entering the building again, and prepared for an immediate exit if they were assaulted once more, but nothing happened.

Ben Resnick stroked his chin, deep in thought, and his brown eyes danced rapidly across a set of graphs displayed on a large, high-definition computer monitor on the table. He was a little less than average in height, had brown hair a few shades darker than his son's, and often looked a bit unkempt. He was also widely regarded as one of the best physicists in the world.

"I'm pretty sure I know what caused this," he said at last. "But I need to check something." He quickly went around the room, cluttered with human equipment and numerous alien devices of every type that he was studying, and deposited electronic sensors at equal distances from the table. He then returned to the table and flipped a switch on a piece of human equipment, about the size of a washing-machine, that was sitting beside it.

Nothing happened.

Mr. Resnick studied the computer screen for several long seconds, nodded, and then flipped the switch the other way.

"I was right," he said triumphantly. "I know what happened." He pointed to the large device he had just switched on and off with no apparent effect. "The ultrasonic generator caused it."

"The what?" said Regan.

"Ultrasonic generator. I was calibrating it when you came in. It generates high frequency sound waves."

"Sound waves? Then why didn't we hear anything?" asked Regan.

"Ultrasound is high frequency sound beyond the range of human hearing. You can't tell if this generator's on without sensors and a computer."

"I don't get it," said Ryan. "Sound that you can't hear? In my book, if you can't hear it, it's not sound. What's the point?"

His father shook his head. "There are far more uses for ultrasonic sound than you would imagine, Ryan. The waves can be very high-energy. You can use them to break up kidney stones. You can bounce them off a fetus to visualize it inside its mother." He raised his eyebrows. "And if you direct powerful enough ultrasonic energy at a liquid, you can even create tiny bubbles that can reach temperatures above those found on the surface of the sun."

"Really?" said Regan.

"I wouldn't kid you," said Mr. Resnick, smiling. "Anyway, the generator was on a setting that should have been harmless. But something in the material of this building somehow concentrated all of the ultrasonic energy exactly where you two entered. Everywhere else in the room was perfectly safe."

Mr. Resnick lowered his head and frowned deeply. He had been so sure what he was doing was harmless, but it had nearly ended in disaster. As careful as he thought he was being, he was clearly not being careful enough. "I can't tell you how sorry I am about this," he said softly to his kids, the horror he felt at having been the cause of something that had severely hurt his children etched in every line on his face. "If I had even thought this was a *possibility* . . . I mean if there was even a chance . . . I never would have—"

"It's okay, Dad," interrupted Ryan. "It was a freak accident. You didn't know this would happen. We'll be fine."

Their father let out a heavy sigh and gave each of them a quick hug.

"Well, as much as I'd like to figure out why this happened," he said, "I won't have the time for at least a few months. But don't worry—I won't be using this generator again until I do."

Regan nodded. "Well, now that that's over," she said, "What's going on with the team?"

The kids were in school during weekdays and missed the daily team meetings, so their parents were responsible for keeping them informed of new developments.

"Quite a lot, actually," replied her mother. "We voted to significantly increase the number of scientists on the project. Everyone is feeling overwhelmed. There's just too much here to study. This place could keep a million scientists busy for a thousand years."

"What about security?" asked Ryan.

"Good question," said Amanda Resnick. "The more people who know the secret the more chance it will leak. And that would be dangerous. If the city's advanced technology got into the wrong hands it would be a disaster. On the other hand, being severely shorthanded while we explore the city is dangerous also. We start to get sloppy. And I don't have to remind you what could happen if we're not careful: the same thing that would happen to a caveman who started playing with a bunch of nuclear warheads," she finished grimly. "And we just witnessed that we can't even always be sure what *Earth* technology will do in here."

"So is Dr. Harris okay with adding more scientists?" asked Ryan.

"Yes, and he's already convinced the president to approve it."

"How many will be on the team altogether?" asked Regan.

"Eventually, almost nine hundred," answered their mother. "Which will make it a very difficult challenge, indeed, for Carl to keep the secret from getting out. But this is a risk we believe we have to take. As it is, we're extremely lucky to have someone like Carl heading up security."

"Absolutely," agreed their father. "Most scientists aren't big fans of military types, but Carl is truly a good man and he's put together a fantastic team. If anyone can maintain security in a humane way, he can. He'll be adding people to the security team as well."

Their mother nodded. "So that's the first piece of big news," she said. She pulled an object from her lab coat that looked like a fat pen with a small isosceles triangle at its tip and three small buttons down its side. "And here is the second." As she moved the object it changed colors. She held it up. "Pamela Joy, our head of chemistry, found three of these early this week in a building near the entrance, and we've been studying them."

Ryan and Regan remained silent, waiting for her to continue.

"It seems to be some sort of portable med-kit." She pointed to the top button. "This button controls the accelerated wound healing function. Think of the triangle on the end of the device as an arrow. Point it at a cut or other wound and press the button for just a second and the wound heals at many times the normal rate. We don't know how, but it's able to speed up cell growth in the region of the injury. The triangle will glow when you press the button so you'll know it's working."

Both kids nodded, clearly fascinated.

"The middle button is for pain relief. Point it at your body, anywhere, and your entire body will be completely free of all pain for about thirty minutes. There may be a way to extend the effect but we haven't found it. If you continue to need pain relief you can just point it at yourself and press the button again."

Amanda Resnick paused and pointed to the lowest button. "This button eradicates infections. Nearly instantly. We've managed to test it on the viruses responsible for colds and the flu, and several nasty bacterial strains, and it's worked like a charm on all of them. Whether it's effective for other human illnesses or alien infections, we don't know yet."

"Very, very cool," said Ryan simply.

"The color change is the opposite of a chameleon, isn't it?" guessed Regan in fascination.

Her parents both nodded proudly. "Exactly right," said her father. "Chameleons change color to match their surroundings so it's more difficult for predators to see them. This device does exactly the opposite. It was

34

designed to stand out—probably to make it harder for someone to lose."

"Watch this," said their mother as she put the pen next to her white lab coat. It immediately turned pitch black. She put it next to the base of the computer screen, which was black, and it instantly turned white. She held it next to a number of different colors and patterns and it always managed to find a counter-color or counter-pattern that made it stand out. Although it was a small device, it seemed to jump out at you regardless of the background it was on.

"Wow," said Regan appreciatively. "Any way to do that with Dad's car keys?"

"That's a cheap shot," said Mr. Resnick, pretending to be hurt. "Besides, I always manage to find them in the end."

"Eventually," said Ryan, rolling his eyes.

Their mother smiled and pulled a second of the pen-like medical devices from her pocket. She handed one to each of her children who examined them with great interest.

"Take good care of those," said Mr. Resnick. "They're yours."

"I don't understand," said Ryan. "I thought you said the team only found three of these?"

"So far, yes," said their mother. "But the team voted unanimously to give these two to you."

"But that's not fair to the team," complained Regan. "We don't expect special treatment just because we're kids."

"Believe me, the way you handled yourself when you joined the team and the way you've handled yourself since, no one thinks you need it. Think of it more as a sign of affection than a sign that you need special treatment."

"We really appreciate it," said Ryan. "But we can't accept these," he insisted. Regan shook her head in agreement beside him.

"The vote was unanimous," said Ben Resnick sternly, in a voice that harbored no dissent. "If you want to be part of the team you have to abide by its votes. You two still get your vote, of course, but this won't change the result. Besides," continued their father, "we're on the lookout for more of these, and I'm sure we'll find some soon."

Ryan stared at his parents for a long moment and knew he wouldn't win this argument. "Well, thanks," he said in surrender. "I guess we can't refuse." He paused. "But I want you to know something," he added. "We really are being very careful inside this city and I'm sure that we'll never need to use them."

But even as he said this, the phrase, "warning, unauthorized entry," flashed across his mind, and he was unable to shake the feeling of unease that had managed to settle over him with surprising intensity.

CHAPTER 5

Security Sweep

Ryan and Regan left their parents and made their way to Carl's security headquarters within the city, located in a building very near the entrance. The building projected a different holographic image around itself every day so that it never looked the same twice. Today it was light-purple and oval shaped.

The siblings entered and found Carl moments later, in civilian clothing but heavily armed, working busily at a computer. He was a handsome man with a square jaw, and his short brown hair had a touch of silver on both sides. Although he was fifty, he was in fantastic shape and carried himself with the athletic ease of a much younger man.

He looked up when they entered and smiled. "Hi guys. How's it going?"

"Good," said Ryan. "Do you have a few minutes?"

"For you two, absolutely. I'm pretty busy, but this is a good time for a break."

Carl walked over to a small, oak roundtable by his desk and plopped into one of the cushioned black chairs surrounding it. He motioned for the kids to join him.

"We heard the team will be growing to nine hundred scientists soon," said Ryan, sitting.

Carl nodded grimly.

"Are you worried about that? Do you think the secret of Prometheus will get out?"

"I've always believed that, Ryan," replied Carl without hesitation. "Eventually. Not to mention," he added with an amused twinkle in his eye, "that it already has."

"It has?" said Ryan in surprise.

"How quickly you forget," mused Carl. "The secret did get out—to you and Regan. We're all lucky it did, but you weren't supposed to know about Prometheus. No other unauthorized parties have learned the secret since, but it's bound to happen again. When it does, I'm confident I'll know about it, but what then? Will I put innocent people who learn of the secret in prison? Will I just swear them to secrecy and trust them? They all won't be worthy of joining the team like the two of you were." He paused. "The good news is that I think I'm nearing a possible solution—it's not perfect but it's the best one I've been able to come up with."

"Great," said Ryan. "What is it?"

"If someone discovers the city, just erase all their memories of it."

"Can you do that?" said Ryan.

"Well, not exactly. You can't isolate just Prometheus memories and leave all the rest alone. The brain has multiple ways of storing, processing and retrieving memories, and they seem to be stored throughout the brain rather than in a precise location. Even the best neuroscientists in the world aren't exactly sure how human memory works."

"I didn't realize it was that tricky."

Carl nodded. "It can be weird, too. I learned about one experiment they did in the 1950's I think you'll like." He leaned in closer. "It began like this: scientists trained a bunch of worms to—"

"You can train a worm?" interrupted Ryan.

Carl shrugged. "Well, I'm not a scientist, but from what I've been told, yes, you can train a worm. Not to fetch your slippers or anything," he added wryly, "but to go toward a light and perform other simple tasks like that." He paused. "Anyway, after the worms were trained, the scientists ground them up and fed them to other, untrained worms."

"Disgusting," said Regan, making a face. "Worms will really eat their friends?"

Carl shrugged his shoulders. "Apparently. I guess the secret is to grind them up into a paste."

"Thanks," said Regan wryly. "I'll be sure to remember that."

"Go on," prompted Ryan, completely fascinated by this bizarre experiment.

Carl smiled. "Believe it or not, they found that after the untrained worms ate the trained ones, they learned the same tasks faster than normal. The knowledge in the brains of the trained worms was somehow passed to the brains of untrained worms." He paused. "Maybe cannibals have the right idea after all," he joked.

"Well, as long as they only eat really smart people," said Regan, smiling.

"I don't know," said Ryan. "I think I'd rather just study harder and skip the whole cannibalism thing."

Carl laughed. "Anyway, getting back to the original subject," he said, "we can't erase Prometheus memories only, but we think we can erase all memories of a specific block of time. This is what happens to people who have something called retrograde amnesia. They suffer a trauma and forget everything that happened to them just prior to the trauma, but their memories are perfectly normal other than that. We think we'll be able to mimic this effect."

Ryan raised his eyebrows questioningly. "We?"

"A group of top neuroscientists at Proact have been working on this for some time. I've been following their progress very closely. They don't know about Prometheus, of course, but they know I'm responsible for their funding. I've been meeting with them fairly regularly for some time now." He glanced at his watch. "In fact, I'm meeting with them in five hours."

"In five hours? That's after ten on a Friday night," noted Ryan.

Carl nodded. "It was the only time we could fit it in. They think they've made a breakthrough. They tell me they've perfected a chemical formula for an inhalant that will do the trick. They think it will erase all memory of the previous ten hours or so."

"Considering everything, I think it's a great idea," said Regan.

"Yeah. It's a lot better than putting someone who discovers the secret in a prison cell in Alaska somewhere," agreed her brother.

Regan smiled and added, "I'm just glad you didn't have this when we first discovered Prometheus."

Carl grinned. "Me too," he said warmly. "Me too." He paused, and his expression became more serious. "So what did you want to see me about?"

"Go ahead," broadcast Ryan telepathically.

"You first."

Ryan took a deep breath and let it out slowly. "You or your men didn't happen to see or hear anything strange in the last few hours, did you?"

Carl laughed. "Strange? You mean other than an alien city and everything inside it?"

Ryan groaned. Maybe he should try that again.

"What I mean is . . . well . . . you didn't happen to hear any kind of warning or . . . I don't know . . . see anyone who shouldn't be here?"

Carl furrowed his brow. "Nooo," he said slowly, trying to figure out where this was headed. "Why do you ask? Did you?"

Ryan frowned. He wished he could just tell him the truth about the warning. If only it hadn't been transmitted telepathically. "Actually, Regan and I thought we saw someone just a little while ago. We only saw him for a second, but he looked a little strange, like he might be an alien."

Carl leaned forward in his seat. "Alien? Really?" He paused in thought. "But you were the ones who learned from the Qwervy that this city is off limits to alien species. Other than vegetation, we haven't seen any alien life whatsoever since we've been here."

"We know," said Regan. "But we really think we saw something."

Carl nodded. "Okay, what did he look like?"

Ryan changed position in his seat, a look of frustration on his face. "We're not really sure. We didn't get a good look at his face. So I guess it could have been a female for all we know. Anyway, the way he, or she, was moving was different—non-human somehow."

"Right," echoed Regan.

"Are you positive it wasn't someone on the team? There are holographic effects all over the city and strangely lit buildings. You catch someone at a strange angle in a strange light and your eyes can play tricks on you."

"We can't be *absolutely* certain," said Ryan. "But we don't think it was someone from the team."

Regan nodded her agreement beside him.

"Boy, are we looking lame," complained Ryan telepathically.

"We don't have a choice," responded Regan.

"Look," said Carl. "The president is coming for a visit in the next week or two. Just prior to this visit I have to meet aboveground, face-to-face, with the Secret Service to assure them that Prometheus is totally secure. They won't give the all clear for the president to leave the White House and make the short trip here in his helicopter, Marine One, until I do."

"Cool," said Regan. "When is he coming?"

Carl frowned. "I hate to do this, but I can't tell nonsecurity members of the team the exact date—except for Dr. Harris, of course. It's on a need to know basis." He paused. "The point is that before I meet with the Secret Service, we'll be doing the most comprehensive security sweep of Prometheus we've ever done. If there's an alien hiding out in this city, we'll be sure to find him."

Ryan knew that the security chief wasn't taking their concern seriously in the least. If he really thought there might be an intruder, he would never be satisfied with waiting a week or two to conduct a search. "That's great,

Carl," said Ryan. "But is there any way you could do a sweep now, even just a quick one? I know we're not giving you much to go on, but I'm asking you to trust us."

Carl stared at Ryan for a long, long time. Ryan met his steady gaze without blinking. Finally, his eyes still locked on Ryan, Carl stood and said, "If you were any other kids in the world, I wouldn't do it. But you and Regan have earned the right to be taken seriously."

"So you'll check it out?" said Ryan, relieved.

Carl nodded. "I'll check it out. I'll have four or five of my men do a sweep. It won't be as thorough as the sweep we'll do to satisfy the Secret Service, but if there's an alien in this city, we should be able to find him by the end of the night. We have vehicles loaded with equipment that can pick up heat signatures and movement."

"Thanks, Carl," said Regan.

"Yeah, we can't tell you how much we appreciate it," added Ryan.

"It's okay," said Carl. "I know you're only looking out for the security of the team." He picked up a sleek walkie-talkie from off his desk, preparing to contact his men. "If your alien generates heat or moves, we'll be able to find him," he said confidently. "I guarantee it."

CHAPTER 6

Sleepover

Ryan and Regan stepped off the Prometheus elevator Saturday morning to find Lieutenants Miguel Sanchez and Cam Kincaid standing guard. Miguel was dark-haired and baby-faced while Cam was tall and thin with straw-colored hair and pale blue eyes.

"Hello kids," they both said in unison.

Both kids returned the greeting.

"Did either of you hear anything about a security sweep last night?" asked Ryan.

Cam nodded. "Not only did I hear about it, I was part of it."

"Did anyone find anything?" asked Ryan eagerly.

"Absolutely nothing," said Cam, shaking his head. "And I was the last to finish, too, so I should know. I got the short straw last night and was assigned the biggest area to cover. Didn't finish up 'till after midnight."

"What time did your shift begin this morning?" asked Regan.

"Five," he answered.

"Wow. That stinks," she said sympathetically. "I'm really sorry."

"Nothing for you to be sorry about. You had nothing to do with it."

"Well, maybe nothing to do with you getting the short straw," agreed Regan. "But I am sorry that Ryan and I called a false alarm."

Cam looked completely confused. "What are you talking about? What false alarm?"

"You know," said Regan, looking sheepish. "We thought we saw something weird, so we asked Carl to do a security sweep."

"Really?" said Cam, raising his eyebrows. "*You* asked for the security sweep. Carl didn't mention that last night, and this morning he was acting very strangely. He's working offsite for a few days, but could you do me a favor: the next time you see him, could you remind him that *you* requested the sweep."

Regan glanced at her brother with a confused look on her face. "Remind him?" she said. "We won't need to *remind* him. We had a very long conversation about it."

"Well he doesn't remember it, that's for sure. Unless he's pulling some kind of strange practical joke. Since I was the last one done, I collected everyone else's reports last night to give to him this morning. He looked at the reports and asked me why we had wasted so much man-power doing a sweep. I reminded him that he was the one who had ordered it. And do you know what he said?"

Both kids shook their heads no.

"He said he didn't know what I was talking about. Why would he order a sweep? He said he was busy but that when he got back from his meetings in a few days he wanted to get to the bottom of this."

The Resnick kids were speechless. This wasn't like Carl at all. He couldn't possibly have forgotten about their visit, so what was he doing? The answer hit them both at the same time.

Regan exchanged a knowing glance with her brother and said, "I think I know what's going on. Did Carl ever tell you he was working on a project with some Proact scientists?"

"Yeah. The memory thing."

"Exactly."

"I know all about it. It's his pet project."

"Well, he was going to meet with them late last night. They thought they found a chemical formula that would erase memory. From what you've said about Carl, they must have been right."

"Are you saying that he tested it on himself?"

Regan nodded. "He probably wanted to try it for himself before he gave it to anyone else. Or else he did it by accident. Either way, he'll be really excited that it works so well."

Cam was visibly relieved. "That would explain it," he said. "I was worried he was going batty. But this is great news."

Miguel had been silent up until this point, but had followed the conversation with great interest. He agreed with Carl that having the ability to erase memory could be of critical importance in maintaining secrecy. "Did Carl tell you the time-frame of the memory wipe?" He asked.

"About ten hours," replied Ryan.

Miguel nodded. "Well, it's a start. Hopefully they can come up with a version that can reach further back. A memory wipe of a few days would give us a lot more breathing room."

The siblings finished their conversation with the two guards and entered Prometheus once again, feeling far better about things than they had the day before. The strange telepathic warning had turned out to be a false alarm and Carl's team of neuroscientists had been successful. They still felt uneasy by the absence of any sign of the Teacher in their minds, but they were getting used to it and there was nothing they could do about it in any case. Perhaps the Qwervy didn't approve of the Teacher maintaining even this slight connection with them.

They stayed in the city as much as they could the entire weekend, as usual, and were exhausted getting up for school on Monday morning. It was a busy week at school and they were only able to visit Prometheus twice during the week, and only for short periods. They never even had the chance to thank Carl for doing the sweep.

Finally, Friday came and they immediately headed to the city. They had been there for only an hour when their parents announced that they all needed to leave.

"Sorry kids," said their mom. "We forgot to tell you. We've invited several key Proact scientists to the house tonight for dinner. We want to get to know them before deciding if we should ask them to join the team."

Ryan groaned. He and his sister had just arrived! And they had plans for later on. He decided not to give up without a fight. "When are you coming back in the morning?"

"Early," said their father. "Probably around six. Why?"

"Regan and I offered to help Dr. Meadows with some experiments tonight," he complained. "And you know we'll just be in the way at your dinner. So I was thinking . . . what if Regan and I spent the night here? You could wake us up when you got back in the morning."

"Absolutely not," snapped their mother immediately. "Under no circumstances am I letting you stay in this city overnight by yourselves."

"We're hardly alone, Mom," argued Ryan. "Everyone here knows us. And we'll be protected by the highest level of security on the planet. We'll be safer here than at home."

"Please, Mom," chimed in Regan. "We could stay

here—in your lab. You have cots in the next room and a refrigerator loaded with food. You and Dad practically live here."

Recently their parents had put in a makeshift sink and all four family members now even had spare tooth-brushes in the alien building.

"What experiments is Dr. Meadows planning?" asked their father.

"He's gonna study the walkway," said Ryan.

The team's first discovery upon entering the city had been a walkway that was made of a super-springy material that catapulted a person forward in a perfectly controlled fashion, greatly accelerating their pace.

"He wants to do a bunch of things," continued Ryan, "like putting sensors on us while we walk on it so he can record exactly what happens. We promised we'd help him."

Ben Resnick pursed his lips together in thought. "They do make some good arguments, Amanda," he said. "And we did forget to tell them we were leaving early tonight. I'm sure Dr. Meadows is counting on their help."

"What if we promise to stay with Dr. Meadows the whole time?" pressed Ryan. "Until we're ready for bed. Then we can just come back here and sleep on the cots. You can wake us up early tomorrow when you get back and we can tell you all about the results."

"You told us you didn't think we needed special

treatment because we're kids," added Regan. "Were you just saying that?"

Amanda Resnick looked into the eyes of her husband and two children and knew she was beaten. She shook her head. "This is against my better judgment, but I suppose we could try it—just this once."

"Thanks, Mom," said both kids happily.

"I suppose you want us to bring a change of clothes for you tomorrow morning as well?"

"That would be great," said Ryan. "You won't regret this. You're the best, Mom."

"Sure," said Mrs. Resnick wryly. "The best. I'm sure I'll win the mother-of-the-year award for agreeing to let my children spend the night without their parents in an extremely dangerous alien city."

Ryan smiled. "It's not that bad," he said.

"Yeah," added Regan. "It's a single night. And you'll be back here for us early in the morning." She looked at her mother reassuringly. "Really, Mom, just how dangerous could it possibly be?"

CHAPTER 7

Invaded

Regan awoke, yawned, and rubbed her eyes. She was wearing the same jeans and lavender t-shirt she had worn the night before, and her hair was pulled back into a ponytail. She was looking forward to telling her parents about the experiments they had conducted with Dr. Meadows the night before. Not only had they learned more about the walkway, but surprisingly, they had learned more about the nanobots as well.

These tiny robots, which looked like mutant ants with the teeth and attitude of piranha, had become quite a nuisance in the early days. Their incessant repairing of things drove the scientists crazy.

One of the most time honored strategies for learning how something worked was to take it apart—carefully. If you didn't know what a television was or how it worked, you could remove a part. If it continued to display a great picture but you couldn't change the volume, the part you removed most likely had something to do with volume control. With enough time, care, and patience you could learn quite a lot. Molecular biologists even used this strategy to learn the function of different genes. They knocked out individual genes in mouse embryos and then studied what happened. Did the embryo still grow into a mouse? If it did, were there any changes in the mouse? What were the changes? If a mouse was born without a tail, the gene that had been eliminated might be involved in tail growth in some way. Scientists had made considerable progress over the years using this strategy.

But the nanobots made this impossible. Remove a part from an alien television to see what effect this would have and the nanobots would repair it instantly, ruining the experiment. Soon some of the scientists, no longer terrified of the nanobots, tried to cover artifacts they didn't want fixed with their bodies so the nanobots couldn't get to them. Surprisingly, this worked. Not only did the nanobots retreat, they would never attempt to repair the object again, even if additional damage was later done to it.

It didn't take long for the scientists to discover that the nanobots were learning from experience. Their programming was truly remarkable. Within days, the scientists didn't have to actively block items they didn't want repaired, the nanobots could somehow tell if the damage was done by accident or for experimental purposes—perhaps by reading the scientists' body language. If done for experimental purposes, the nanobots would completely ignore the item, not even swarming in the first place. If the damage was done accidentally, they were their old reliable selves, making quick and perfect repairs.

But last night this changed. Dr. Matthews had cut a piece from the walkway for experimental purposes, but the nanobots swarmed anyway. Dr. Matthews was forced to actively try to stop them, something that had not been necessary for some time, but even this didn't work. They politely, but persistently, worked around him until they finished their repairs, undeterred by his actions. Why had this happened? Dr. Matthews wasn't sure yet, but his working hypothesis was that since the walkway was for public use, the nanobots could not ignore damage done to it, no matter what the reason.

Not for the first time Regan marveled at the wonders of this amazing city. There was no doubt in her mind that she and Ryan were the luckiest kids on Earth.

She glanced over at the digital clock on the small table by her cot. It read 8:17.

That was odd.

She toured the laboratory for a few minutes and returned to the cots, pushing Ryan awake.

"Wha . . . wha," he said groggily, opening his eyes just a crack.

Like his sister, he had fallen asleep the night before without bothering to change and was still wearing green cargo pants and a yellow t-shirt. His hair was messy and pointed in several different directions at once.

"Ryan, it's past eight o'clock."

"So?"

"So—Mom and Dad were supposed to be here at least an hour ago."

Ryan rubbed his eyes. "They're probably in the next room and just wanted to let us sleep."

Regan shook her head anxiously. "They're *not*. I checked. No sign that they were here at all this morning."

Ryan pulled his feet onto the floor and sat up. "That's strange. They must have been held up. I'm sure they'll be here any second."

"Just to be on the safe side, let's ask the elevator guards if they saw them."

"Okay," agreed Ryan. "But I'm sure there's nothing to worry about." He grinned mischievously. "And this is our chance to tease Mom and Dad about not being responsible. After all, we were here when we were supposed to be and they weren't."

Regan pretended to smile lightheartedly, but she couldn't shake an uneasy feeling that had settled over her.

After quickly brushing their teeth, they each grabbed a muffin and a small cardboard box filled with orange juice and headed for the golf-cart parked just outside. It was Regan's turn to drive. They drove for several minutes without seeing anyone else, which was unusual. At least a few members of security were always present—day and night. And most scientists entered the city at the crack of dawn and were in full stride already by eight o'clock, even on weekends. But today the city was strangely quiet.

They arrived at the entrance a few minutes later.

At least they should have.

The opening was gone!

Regan gasped, while Ryan's eyes widened in horror.

The alien force-field was perfectly intact. No kaleidoscope of colors that represented an opening in the field. No doorway out of the city and back into the cavern. There was no question they were in the correct location. But where was the opening? The city's only exit was gone!

They were trapped! Just like the first time they had entered the city.

"Impossible," said Ryan, in total disbelief. It was like a very bad dream. How could this be happening *again*. "What's going on?"

Regan said nothing, continuing to stare straight ahead in shock. The last time this exit had disappeared they had been completely alone. At least this time they wouldn't be. She was at least thankful for that.

Her brother must have been thinking the same thing. "We need to find the rest of the team," he said worriedly after a few long seconds of silence. "Even if the entrance closed down at three in the morning there should be at least fifteen people here. Maybe one of them will know what's going on."

They rushed to the nearby building that Carl had selected as his headquarters within the city and went inside.

It was abandoned!

Again, this was *impossible*. There were always at least a few of Carl's people planning and watching security monitors twenty-four hours a day.

They drove to four additional alien structures that had been converted into labs or were actively being studied by members of the team with the same result.

The city was a ghost town. Maybe they were alone, after all.

With each new discovery of abandoned quarters that shouldn't have been abandoned the sick feeling in the pits of their stomachs intensified. Changing their strategy, they drove toward the center of the city, stopping periodically to enter multistory buildings to use as lookouts.

They were each at a different window on the third floor of one such building, silently searching the city below for any signs of life, when Ryan's voice exploded through the silence. "Regan!" he shouted. "Quick."

She raced over and joined her brother who was pointing at something through the window. She looked out in plenty of time to see the reason for his alarm. A chill went down her spine as what she was seeing fully registered. A Hauler was slowly passing the building. They both watched it in shock, their mouths falling open.

Inside the flatbed compartment three men were kneeling, clutching machine guns against their chests expertly with both hands, one hand at the trigger and one hand supporting the butt of the weapon.

The men were dressed from head to toe in black. In addition to black socks, black shoes, and a black jumpsuit, they each wore a thick black nylon belt with a variety of black pouches and gear clipped on, and a black ski cap. They each faced a different direction, carefully scanning the city as the vehicle slowly advanced, their intensity and alertness unmistakable even at a distance. There could be no doubt that these were superbly trained and extremely dangerous men.

Inside the large driving compartment were two more of the black-clad men, one driving and the other pointing a machine gun at a man in civilian clothes, handcuffed to a thick steel pole running across the back of the compartment.

It was Cam Kincaid!

And he was clearly a prisoner.

If there had been any doubt before, there was none now.

Prometheus had been invaded!

CHAPTER 8

Spies

Things had quickly gone from bad to worse.

They watched from the window as the vehicle passed a powerful waterfall that gushed from the top of a nearby building and slammed into a shallow pool far below. The water seemed to appear from nowhere and lead nowhere, but this was because the waterfall didn't really exist. It was a perfect holographic simulation, utterly realistic, right down to the roar of crashing water. The Hauler came to a gleaming, arch-shaped structure about fifty yards away, just beyond the waterfall, and stopped. The structure was bright gold in color, and the two tapering legs of the arch were joined together by a rectangular building that shimmered, as though its walls had melted and were forever flowing around it like molten metal. All five of the black-clad figures jumped out, with the one in front prodding Cam roughly forward with the butt of his assault rifle.

Moments later they disappeared inside the rectangular structure, except for two of the men who stationed themselves on either side of the door with their rifles at the ready.

Ryan shook his head violently to break out of his near-paralysis. "How could these guys have made it through security?" he whispered. "It's just not possible."

"I don't know," said Regan. "But anyone who could do it has to be incredibly dangerous."

"Thanks. That makes me feel a lot better," said Ryan wryly, but he knew she was right. "Okay, so they've taken Cam prisoner. Where is everyone else?"

As Regan considered his question her eyes went wide and such a horrified expression came over her face that Ryan instantly knew what she was thinking. She was clearly thinking the worst.

"I don't think they're dead," he said softly, trying to reassure her. "We didn't see blood or any evidence of that anywhere. Cam is handcuffed but other than that they didn't hurt him."

Regan considered her brother's argument, and while still unsettled, brightened visibly. "In that case, since we haven't been able to find anyone, those soldiers probably already captured everyone else and brought them to that building," she said, nodding her head in its direction.

"Yeah. That makes sense. Those guys were on a

hunting expedition. Searching for anyone they missed the first time around."

Regan nodded gloomily.

Ryan paused for a long moment in thought before coming to an inescapable conclusion. "We need to spy on them," he said finally.

Regan sighed heavily. "I had a feeling you were going to say that," she said.

"Unless we learn what's going on as soon as possible, we don't have a chance."

"We might not have a chance anyway. And we might get caught while we're trying to spy."

"Maybe. But I think we need to risk it. Besides, we're in luck. I know every inch of the building they're in."

"Really?" said Regan, surprised. "I've never seen it before."

"Dad and I practically lived there that weekend you were busy helping Mom study some of the zoo planets. There's just a single, rectangular room inside, completely surrounded by a narrow corridor. They must have set up headquarters in the main room."

"What were you and Dad doing in there?"

Ryan raised his eyebrows. "You know the ceramic samples Dad is always studying?"

"The superconductors?"

Ryan nodded. "He got them from inside that building."

Regan's eyes widened. Her father considered this to

be among his most important projects. A superconductor was a material through which electricity could flow without losing any energy at all. This was extremely rare. The only superconductors Earth scientists had developed would only work at icy temperatures far below zero. But the material their dad had found would work at room temperature, something that could revolutionize such things as computer technology and the generation of electricity.

"The inner walls of that building are made of a complex ceramic material. Once Dad realized they were superconductors, I couldn't get him to leave; even to eat. He spent the entire weekend there doing experiments and taking samples from the walls."

"Okay," said Regan. "So you do know the building well. But how does that help us?"

"While Dad was working, I did some exploring. Along with the one entrance you can easily see in the front, I found an invisible doorway on the other side of the building. It leads to the hallway surrounding the central room." His eyes blazed with determination. "Once we're in the hallway we should be able to hear what's going on in the other room. Even better, if I'm remembering right, the samples Dad cut from the walls left small holes that we should be able to look through."

"Great," said Regan, frowning. The set-up her brother described really was as perfect for spying as they could possibly hope for, which left them no excuse not to do what he was proposing. "Lucky us," she mumbled unhappily.

"We can *do* this, Regan," he said confidently. "All we have to do is make it through the invisible door without being seen."

Regan peered cautiously out of the window once again. The guards were stationed at the front entrance only. If they snuck up from behind, they really should be able to make it to the hallway.

"Okay," she said as bravely as possible. "What are we waiting for?"

Keeping out of the guards' line of sight, they drove back the way they had come for several miles and then circled back so they could approach the structure from behind. They abandoned the golf-cart behind a small cylindrical building about sixty yards from their target and cautiously closed the remaining distance on foot. They crouched low as they approached, keeping out of sight behind exotic vegetation and a few Haulers parked haphazardly behind the structure.

Finally, they were at their destination. A section of the flowing gold wall dutifully vanished as they approached and moments later they were inside the hall surrounding the central building.

They had made it!

Regan's heart beat like a jackhammer, so loudly that if she didn't know better, she would have sworn that everyone in the building could easily hear it as it pounded explosively against the walls of her chest. Ryan's pulse matched his sister's beat for beat and his stomach churned nervously.

While they could hear chatter from the main room quite clearly, several people were talking at once and they couldn't make out anything specific being said.

Ryan motioned his sister to follow him. He gestured to a series of quarter-sized holes bored through the smooth, bright-orange wall about a foot off the ground, evenly spaced about every ten feet. *"Dad's samples,"* explained Ryan telepathically.

All they needed to do was lie on their stomachs and line up one eye with a hole and they would both be able to observe the entire main room. So far, so good.

Regan felt an odd tingle in her brain. She had the feeling it was a telepathic signal, but a very faint one. Was it the Teacher trying to contact them? If so, the Teacher was weaker than ever and was using a strange frequency that didn't quite work.

"Do you feel that?" she broadcast to her brother.

"Yes. Could it be the Teacher?" asked Ryan.

"I don't know," she replied.

Ryan was about to broadcast something else when he was stopped cold by an eerie sixth-sense.

He froze! What was that?

Ryan strained, his senses extended to their farthest

possible limits. He heard an incredibly faint, but unmistakable, shuffle coming from directly behind him!

Someone—or some thing—had snuck up on them.

Ryan remained perfectly still, just able to fight off his instinctive urge to almost literally jump out of his skin. His stomach was in knots and the tiny hairs on the back of his neck were standing on end. *"Regan, behind us,"* he alerted his sister telepathically.

But as he was about to wheel around to face whatever was approaching, he felt hot breath on the back of his neck, and he knew with a horrible certainty that he had waited too long.

CHAPTER 9

Captured

Before Ryan or Regan could even think about moving a pair of giant hands lashed out from behind them, one clamping itself firmly over each of their mouths. Their startled grunts were entirely muffled by the large hand. Ryan fought for control and while doing so finally caught a glimpse of his assailant.

It was Dan Walpus! *Captain* Dan Walpus. He was wearing civilian clothes as usual—tan slacks and a blue knit shirt—but a military assault rifle was slung over his shoulder.

Regan recognized him an instant later and both she and Ryan immediately ceased struggling.

What a relief!

Dan caught each of their eyes and gave them a reassuring nod and then gestured with his head in the direction of the main room. They nodded back, letting him know that they would stay quiet. He gently removed his hands from around their mouths and crouched down to their level. "Sorry," he whispered, so quietly they weren't sure if they were hearing it or reading his lips. "If I just tapped you on your backs you might have called out in surprise and given away our position. Had to do it this way."

"What's happening?" whispered Regan.

"Not sure," mouthed Dan. "But I'm the only adult not captured. I was doing reconnaissance when I saw you and decided to follow. Glad I did. Didn't know about the back-door access to this building." He looked around and spotted the quarter-sized holes in the wall. "Very glad I did," he remarked with a slight smile.

Dan removed the rifle from around his neck and propped it gently against the wall. "I'll watch from this position," he whispered. He pointed to the next two small holes in the wall that appeared at ten-foot intervals. "You man those. We need to learn as much as we can. If I think I have a chance to take them out at any point, I'll signal you. If I do, I want you out of the building. Quickly and quietly. No hesitation, no argument. I will not have you in this building when the shooting starts. Is that understood?"

Both kids nodded.

"Good."

They spread out, each lying on the floor. They cautiously put their eyes to the holes, slowly enough so no one in the other room could possibly catch any movement.

Against the far wall of the main room, about twenty scientists were huddled together on the floor, bound and gagged. Regan fought off an inadvertent gasp.

Two of the captives were her parents!

They didn't look injured, nor, fortunately, did any of the other captives. The hands and ankles of each captive were bound together with thin, but extremely tough, strips of black plastic. These plasticuffs, also referred to as zip-strips, were currently in favor with Special Forces teams because they were light, easy to carry, extremely fast and extremely effective. They resembled tie strips used to bind bundles of electrical cable. A soldier could pull a zip-strip from his belt, wrap it around an enemy's wrists, insert the end in something resembling a tiny, hard plastic belt loop that was attached to it, and pull. Small teeth in the strip would ratchet it to the desired tightness in seconds. Unlike metal handcuffs, there was no lock mechanism to pick. They could only be removed if someone cut through the ultra-hard plastic, a surprisingly difficult task. It was virtually impossible for a prisoner to free themselves from these restraints.

Carl and seven of his men were separated from the scientists, and each also had their hands behind their backs, their wrists locked tightly together with plasticuffs and their ankles bound in the same way.

In the middle of the room, five enemy soldiers were

milling about. When they spoke it was in low tones and they appeared to be waiting for something. A few minutes later it became clear what when an imposing, black-clad soldier entered the room. He was unmistakably different from the others. He was unusually pale and towered over everyone in the room, including some of Carl's men who were well over six feet tall.

As he entered the soldiers stopped talking and a hush fell over the room. He looked around and scowled. "There's still one man left to collect," he barked. "Were you all planning to just stand around here all day!" he demanded.

"You assured us that you would locate him yourself once he regained consciousness," protested a soldier who was as thick as a tree trunk and looked strong enough to lift a car. "If you like, we can send out another search party."

The tall man radiated an unmistakable air of authority. "No, Captain Hanly," he said, calming down. "That won't be necessary. He isn't going anywhere. I'll get him myself in due course."

He walked up to where the members of Prometheus security were tightly bound and lying on the ground and pulled Carl roughly up off the floor. The head of security looked small in the giant's grasp. After he was let go, it took Carl several seconds to steady himself on feet that were bound tightly together. Once he was balanced, the newcomer pulled the gag roughly from his mouth.

"So this is the great Colonel Carl Sharp," said the tall, pale soldier, sneering. "It's my understanding that while Dr. Harry Harris is in charge of this entire project, *you* are in charge when there is any threat to security." He raised his eyebrows. "Would it be safe to assume that *I* qualify as a threat to security?"

Carl met his captor's eyes unflinchingly. "Who are you?" he said evenly. "And what do you want?"

The man laughed. "I already have what I want. I want this city. I have one last man to capture and then I'll have it completely locked down."

"You are sadly mistaken. I have over twenty men remaining in this city who are planning their attack even as we speak. To secure this city they will consider me and the others expendable. If they can't take you out any other way, they'll bomb this building back into the stone age."

This caused the man to laugh even louder. He stepped forward and stooped until he was directly in Carl's face. "Nice try, Colonel," he growled. "But you can't bluff me. I know everything there is to know about your security. I know the name and background of everyone in this room. And finally, I know Captain Dan Walpus is still at large—the only person in this entire city who is. Once we neutralize him, there won't be anyone left who can stop me. So don't think you can scare me with your imaginary force of twenty men." He smiled cruelly. "You have no idea what you're up against here."

"Then why don't you tell me," said Carl evenly.

"Oh, don't you worry, Colonel," he assured him. "I have every intention of telling you. I wouldn't have it any other way," he added, smirking. "My name," he began, pausing for effect, "is Tezoc Zoron. I come from a planet thousands of light years away called Morca."

The eyes of every Prometheus team member in the room widened, and this would have been accompanied by numerous gasps if not for the gags. Even Carl couldn't help but shrink back in surprise at this announcement.

"What are you doing here?" said Carl, recovering quickly.

"Try not to ask stupid questions, Colonel Sharp. We both know it doesn't take a highly decorated colonel to fathom what I'm doing here."

He paced back and forth in front of Carl, never taking his eyes from him, and continued. "I was a prisoner on my planet for twelve years. Twelve years!" he shouted suddenly. Then, regaining control he added in almost a whisper, "And for the past seven years, do you know what I've been doing?"

Carl remained silent.

"I've been studying your species," he said. "That's what. I've learned everything about you. I know your history, I know your cultures, and I know your technology and military capabilities. I've even learned the English language."

"Okay, so you studied us. So you wanted to take a

vacation here on Earth once your prison sentence expired. Good for you."

"My sentence did not expire!" snapped Tezoc. "I escaped. And despite the fact that my people have all turned into such sheep that their prisons are like luxury resorts, escape is considered impossible. In fact, I'm the only one who has ever escaped a Morcan prison in hundreds of years. I am unique, even on my own planet. I am superior. You should feel honored that I chose to come to this planet."

Carl looked up into the alien's pale blue eyes. "In case you haven't heard, Tezoc, Earth is off limits. When the Qwervy find out you're here, they won't be happy."

"Silence!" shouted Tezoc in rage. "Never mention the name of that putrid race again. Those arrogant fools won't ever find out I'm here. I've planned too carefully. I found a way to escape prison, I found a way to come here, and I found a way to take this planet off their grid. They're so busy sitting in judgment of other species they won't even realize Earth is off the grid for another fifty years, and they won't get around to checking up on it for another hundred." Tezoc's eyes burned with hatred. "And by that time, I'll be ready for them."

"Are these men from your planet also?" Carl asked, gesturing with his head toward the men standing behind Tezoc.

"Don't be ridiculous. Of course not. The men you see here are mercenaries: highly trained soldiers from around the world who sell their services to the highest bidder."

"Thanks for the vocabulary lesson," said Carl sarcastically. "But I know only too well what a merc is," he added distastefully, using the common military abbreviation for a mercenary.

Carl tilted his head in thought. "So you came directly to the city through a portal. But your men didn't. They came from the outside. How did you manage to get them through all the levels of security and take down this city without a single alarm going off? I don't care if you are an alien. I don't care if you have technology that men can only dream of. It's impossible. Maybe we could be breached through the use of sufficiently advanced alien technology—maybe—but not blindsided like this. An entire army couldn't pull it off, let alone a sorry bunch of mercs."

"And yet here we are," said Tezoc, very pleased with himself. "I'm afraid I'm not going to tell you how we did it, Colonel. Think of it as a trade secret."

Carl frowned, not surprised. "Once you breached the city, you knocked us all unconscious somehow. It couldn't have been gas; we were too far spread out for that. How did you do it?"

So that was how they were able to gather up the scientists and Carl's crack security team so quickly and without a fight, thought Ryan from his post in the hallway. Tezoc had put everyone in the city to sleep remotely somehow. He and Regan were *already* asleep at the time and so nothing changed for them. Dan must have also lost consciousness, but they had obviously been unable to find him before he had regained it.

"You know what I'm beginning to think?" said Tezoc. "I'm beginning to think you're trying to keep me talking. I think you're stalling. Waiting for something. Am I right?"

"I don't know what you're talking about," said Carl evenly.

From behind Tezoc one of the mercs raised his rifle and pointed it at Carl's leg. He had an olive complexion and a cruel demeanor, as if he truly enjoyed hurting people. "Play any more games and I'll take out your leg," he said coldly.

Tezoc went berserk, pushing the rifle aside angrily. "What are you doing!" he demanded. "Captain Brice, I'm paying you a king's ransom to follow my orders, not to think for yourself."

He turned to all the mercenaries behind him and pointed at Carl. "If any one of you as much as scratches this man—*ever*—I will kill you in ways so horrible they are beyond your imagination. Is that understood?"

They all quickly made it clear that it was.

"And make sure the two men guarding out front get the message also," snapped Tezoc. He began to pace silently, gathering his thoughts and attempting to calm himself.

Several of the mercs had their backs to the hidden observers peering out through the small holes in the orange wall. One of these, the shortest soldier of them all, had been so totally still the entire time Tezoc was speaking he could have been asleep. But suddenly, he jerked his head to the side. Then, without warning, he wheeled around and fired precisely on Dan's position. His rifle was set on single-shot, and the bullet shattered the ceramic wall in front of Dan, creating a three-foot hole. Dan's assault rifle was knocked from its perch against the wall. The tall captain executed an expert roll and grabbed the weapon from the floor, ready to come up firing, when a second bullet pierced his arm.

Dan's arm jerked backward and his rifle fell to the floor once again as the merc prepared to take a third, and final, shot.

CHAPTER 10

A Deadly Threat

"Freeze!" shouted the merc, his finger pausing on the trigger.

Dan raised his hands in surrender and tilted his head, almost imperceptibly, toward the two siblings. He shook his head, so slightly as to be unnoticeable to anyone but Ryan and Regan, and his eyes burned fiercely, sending them a message they correctly interpreted as, *Don't you dare help me and reveal yourselves.*

Dan kicked his rifle hard, sending it sliding toward the merc, and followed quickly behind it until he was in front of the man who had shot him.

Two other soldiers rushed to either side of the new opening in the orange wall and raised their rifles so they were pointing straight up. They signaled to each other as if trying to time a plunge through the hole.

Ryan and Regan, still hidden from view, realized in

horror that they were seconds from being discovered, but they also knew that if they moved their discovery would be just as certain.

"Stand down!" ordered Tezoc.

"It's standard practice to clear an area after you've found an enemy combatant there," protested one of the men.

"I said stand down. There's no one else there. In fact, there are no other humans in this entire city. I guarantee it. There is no need to clear anything."

The men relaxed their posture, lowered their weapons, and returned to their initial positions.

Inside the hallway, the siblings allowed themselves to breathe for the first time since the incident began. That had been close. Too close. And now Dan was a captive also. Things were looking hopeless.

Tezoc walked over to Dan and studied him as he stood bleeding in the middle of the floor. "Captain Walpus," he said with satisfaction. "Welcome to the party."

He bent down and picked up Dan's assault rifle and handed it to one of his men. "Kicking your weapon, Captain? I thought the United States Special Forces trained their soldiers better than that. You guys are supposed to be the best in the world. I'm disappointed."

Ryan, continuing to watch through the small hole near the bottom of the wall, knew exactly what Dan had done. If the mercenaries had bent over to pick up his weapon where it had fallen, they almost surely would have seen where he and Regan were hiding. Dan had rushed from the hallway for the same reason—to protect them.

The soldiers allowed Dan to tear a thick strip from his shirt and use it as a makeshift bandage on his arm to staunch the flow of blood. The bullet had gone cleanly through the muscle of his upper arm. It was painful, but all things considered, he had been very lucky.

Dan studied the man who had shot him. In addition to his short stature he was quite thin, with a hard look on his face. While all of the other soldiers had long since removed their black knit ski-caps, he was still wearing a hat, except his was a heavy black baseball cap rather than the knit variety initially worn by all the others. The man was very slow and deliberate in his movements. Even so, there was something about him that radiated danger more so than any of the other soldiers. It would be wise to stay clear of this one, no matter how sleepy he appeared. "Your back was turned," said Dan finally. "What gave me away?"

"*I* gave you away," boasted Tezoc before the merc could reply. "I signaled your position to Major Manning here," he said, gesturing to Dan's attacker, "my second in command. He took care of the grunt work of shooting you." He leaned forward. "You see, Captain Walpus, I could sense your brainwaves."

Dan raised his eyebrows. "My brainwaves?"

"I'm sorry, Captain, did I forget to tell your Colonel Sharp that I can sense brainwaves? I'm a bit telepathic as a matter of fact. I would have sensed you earlier but I was preoccupied. That is how I know there are no other humans remaining in the city. If there were, I would sense their minds, no matter how far away."

"How is he missing us?" asked Regan telepathically.

"When the Teacher changed the frequency of our minds so we could communicate with it better, it must have put us on the wrong frequency for this guy to pick up."

"So it wasn't the Teacher we've been feeling against our minds," broadcast Regan in disappointment. *"It was Tezoc."*

"I guess so. That must be why we only felt it when we entered the building."

While the siblings had been communicating, two of the mercs had bound and gagged Dan and had shoved him on the ground with the other prisoners.

"Now where was I?" said Tezoc, turning back to Carl. "Too many interruptions." He paused in thought. "Oh yes, I was saying I suspected you were trying to stall me for some reason. Do you remember?"

Carl nodded. "Yes. And I still have no idea what you're talking about."

"Oh, I think you do," said Tezoc. "Let me help you out. You're waiting for the cavalry to storm in here and rescue you."

Carl said nothing.

"Go on, admit it. As I told you, I know all there is to know about your security. Unless your men upstairs get the proper signal from down here every few hours, they'll check up on things. When they find they can't reach anyone in security down here, they'll investigate further. In no time at all they'll learn what happened and sound the alarm. Within hours they'll have the entire military might of your nation converging on Pennsylvania to storm this city, secret or no secret. Is that about right?"

Rage flashed across Carl's face, but only for an instant. While his eyes still burned like twin lasers, he forced the muscles in his face to relax. He would not let Tezoc know he was scoring points. Once again, Carl chose to remain silent.

"Well I hate to disappoint you," continued Tezoc smugly, "but they won't be coming. I've been planning this for a long time. I'll admit, I had to adjust my plans recently when I discovered that humans had found a way into the city here, but that just made things more interesting. You see, Colonel Sharp, once my men were all inside this city, I closed down your entrance. I fried the equipment you were using to keep the doorway open with a timed, electronic pulse."

Tezoc smiled, quite pleased with himself. "I think we both know what that means. No cavalry will be coming to the rescue, Colonel. All the tanks and jet fighters in the world, even if you could get them this far underground, won't even *scratch* that force-field. No military heroics will get you out of this. Which means that I can use this city as a base of operations for as long as I like. And unlike you, I know how to make use of the technology here."

"Congratulations, Tezoc," said Carl. "You've won yourself a base of operations. But consider this—you've just traded in your prison on Morca for a larger prison here. Even if you brought the technology to reopen the entrance, the military will be waiting for you in the cavern whenever you decide to leave."

"Good point," said Tezoc smoothly. "That's why I'm not exiting through your cavern."

"Where else?" said Carl.

"Since, as you say, all of your forces will be concentrated at the cavern, I plan to stay as far away from it as possible."

Carl shook his head. "So you break through the force-field somewhere else. What good will *that* do you? This city's buried. You'll have nothing but granite and limestone and clay for a mile above you."

"Come now, Colonel, you insult me. Haven't I already demonstrated that I plan very carefully. I know how to use the technology in this city. These cities are all laid out exactly alike. There is equipment here that will allow me to cut through your mile of rock in a single day and emerge far from where anyone would think of looking for me."

Carl fought to stay calm and alert and not dwell on the horrible implications of Tezoc's words. "Well, it appears you've thought of everything," he finally said, grimly, deciding his only remaining hope was to try to get Tezoc to become overconfident and lower his guard.

Tezoc shook his head bitterly. "No, Colonel," he said, frowning. "Not everything. I did make one miscalculation. After I destroyed your entrance, I found that the technology I brought with me to open a hole in the force-field somewhere else isn't working. I'm still not sure why."

"So you're trapped in here, after all," said Carl, brightening visibly.

Tezoc smiled. "Only for a short while, Colonel, only for a short while. It's true that I'm now unable to get back through the force-field. But aren't you forgetting something?"

Carl looked blank.

"Aren't you forgetting that the only man on this planet, including me, who has proven he can get through the shield is in this very room." He pushed the gag back into Carl's mouth. "It's been fun, Colonel, but there is someone else I need right now."

Tezoc walked to the scientists and went straight for

Ben Resnick, pulling him abruptly up off the floor and removing the gag from his mouth.

"Dr. Resnick, how are you? I must say, when I was gathering intelligence for this mission, I was impressed to learn you had managed to get through the Qwervy force-field—and not much impresses me. I need you to do it again."

Ben Resnick did not respond.

Tezoc put his hands in front of him, palms outward, in a gesture of apology. "I'm sorry, I should have said *Mister* Resnick. I forgot. Even though you've earned multiple doctorates in physics you prefer the simple title of Mister. How rude of me."

"Look, ah . . . Tezoc," said Ben Resnick. "Breaching the barrier is impossible. I don't have the proper equipment."

"Oh, don't worry about that," came the calm reply. "I'll make sure you have all the computing power and equipment you need. I'm sure you can measure the frequencies of the force-field on the inside of the city and make any recalculations that are necessary." His tone changed from pleasant to deadly serious. "You have six hours."

"You can't possibly get me to help you, and even if you could, it can't be done in six hours anyway."

Tezoc shrugged. "Well, I hope for their sakes," he said, gesturing to the scientists, "that you're wrong about that. Because in six hours and every hour there-after, if there isn't an opening in the force-field, one of these innocent people is going to die horribly."

Tezoc smiled broadly and leaned in closer to Ben Resnick's face. "Starting with your wife," he whispered ominously.

CHAPTER 11

Planning a Rescue

Ben Resnick shrank back in horror. "How do I know you won't kill us all anyway, even if I succeed?"

"You don't," snapped Tezoc bluntly. "But you and your colleagues are among the most talented scientists on the planet. I might need one of you again someday. You'll just have to take my word that I won't harm any of you. Provided I get full cooperation, of course."

Tezoc made a show of looking at his watch. "You're down to five hours and fifty-nine minutes," he said pointedly. "Ready to start work, or would you like to chat some more?"

The alien didn't wait for a response. He selected three mercenaries. "The four of us will go with Mr. Resnick here to work on our escape," he announced to his other soldiers. "The rest of you stay here and guard the prisoners. Major Manning will be in charge when

I'm not here. Follow his orders as you would mine. The three million dollars I guaranteed each of you is just the beginning. Prove your loyalty to me and the sky's the limit."

After a short telepathic discussion, the kids decided to follow Tezoc and their father. They already knew where the prisoners were being kept. But if they failed to learn where their father was being taken they might not be able to find him again.

Tezoc and his group set out in a green Hauler. The large electric truck was easy for the siblings to see from a great distance and allowed them to lag far behind and still follow in their golf-cart. Not that the soldiers were paying attention to the terrain behind them anyway. Tezoc's mental abilities made them overconfident; certain that the towering alien would detect anyone following them, and just as certain that there was no one left to do so anyway. They surely would have paid far more attention had they known there were two kids in the city who didn't register on their boss's personal radar screen.

The mercenaries stopped against a seemingly random part of the city's barrier and set up camp. Tezoc handed their father a small computer and an object that he could use to measure various forces in the wall and explained their use. He then sent his men, one at a time, on various errands, carefully describing the location and appearance of the equipment he wanted them to gather.

After only thirty minutes, a large table and full complement of chairs from a nearby building had been moved to the site. The table was made from a yellow-colored alien material that was cool to the touch and remarkably smooth. Ben Resnick sat at the table furiously studying data and formulating ever more complex equations for the computer to solve.

A considerable distance away, his two children were carefully peeking around the side of a building, watching.

"Tezoc never leaves Dad's side," whispered Regan. "And there are always at least two of the three soldiers guarding him."

"I think we need to try to rescue him anyway," whispered her brother. "Those men are watching Dad just to make sure he doesn't try to get away. They can't possibly be expecting a rescue attempt. I think we can surprise them."

Regan shook her head. "It's *suicide* Ryan. We wouldn't stand a chance. Plus," she added, "we don't know anything about Tezoc. He could be stronger and faster than he looks."

"We can't just do *nothing* while time runs out," protested Ryan.

"I agree. But if we're going to try a suicidal rescue, let's at least try one that makes sense. Let's go back to the other building and try to rescue the prisoners there. If you count Tezoc, there are four people guarding Dad.

87

That leaves five soldiers at the other building—three inside and two guarding the entrance."

Ryan nodded. "That's right."

"So we'd have to go up against about the same number of soldiers to free Dad or to free the prisoners. But Dad is out in the open, making surprise almost impossible. The prisoners, on the other hand, are in a building that has a secret back-entrance the mercs don't know about. And if we pull it off somehow, it should be easy to free Dad, because then we'll have Carl and his men on our side."

Ryan nodded. "You're right," he said. "You make a lot of sense. So do you have a plan for the rescue?"

"Come on, Ryan," she said with a grin. "I've figured out *who* we should rescue. Just so you don't feel left out, I'll let you decide *how* we should do it."

"I'll take that as a no."

"I don't have any idea," admitted Regan. "But I'm sure you'll be able to figure out something."

"Thanks," said Ryan, rolling his eyes. "I appreciate the confidence," he added miserably.

They tried for several minutes to come up with a rescue plan, but failed to think of any that would give them even a slight chance of success. Finally, they decided to go back to the alien school to see if they could activate the Teacher the way they had the first time. The Teacher had been restricted from helping them, or even speaking with them, but surely in this situation the Qwervy would be willing to make an exception.

They made their way to the school building but were unable to activate the Teacher no matter what they tried. They were disappointed, but not entirely surprised.

They were also keenly aware that the clock was ticking.

They walked to a few solid cubes that were next to each other in the schoolroom and sat down. The instant they sat the cubes became liquid-like and surrounded their bodies in perfect comfort. They felt as if they were floating in warm water, only it was even more soothing, and they didn't bob around or get wet.

"Remember when you sat down on one of these cubes our first day in this city?" said Ryan. "And how surprised you were they turned out to be chairs?"

"Yeah. How could I forget? It was right before we found the Teacher."

Ryan nodded and thought back to that day. Their mother had been near death, the team had vanished, and they thought they might be trapped in the city forever. It had been hopeless. Almost as hopeless as their current situation. But they had never stopped fighting, even for an instant. They had never stopped thinking. They had never given up.

And they would not give up now, vowed Ryan. There had to be a way to rescue the captives. *Think,* he ordered himself. He slapped the palm of his hand gently against his forehead several times in a futile effort to jump-start his brain. *Think!*

He lowered his hand to a small table beside him in total frustration. He was getting nowhere.

But just a few seconds after his hand touched the table his eyes brightened and a smile came over his face. The answer was so simple he was embarrassed he had not thought of it sooner. But then again, answers always seemed obvious once you had found them.

"Regan," he said, his voice more hopeful than it had been in some time now. "I have a plan. We just might be able to pull this off, after all."

CHAPTER 12

Globe Attack

Regan crouched on one side of the hole that Major Manning had shot in the bright-orange ceramic wall. Carefully, she brought the razor-sharp, nine-inch knife she had retrieved from a supply cabinet sideways to her mouth. She clamped down on its blade with her teeth, with the sharp edge pointing away from her. Ryan did the same with an identical knife on the other side of the gap. They felt a slight tingle brushing at their brains, a residual trace of Tezoc's telepathic mental energy still in the building.

"Ready?" broadcast Ryan.

"Ready."

They each carefully removed two fragile glass globes from a bag they had taken from the supply cabinet, holding one in each hand like a pair of giant softballs.

The glass globes had been on each of the tables in

the alien classroom. When Ryan had put his hand on the table he had spotted a globe and remembered the last time he had seen them. He had shattered one, causing the nanobots to swarm out from under the floor. At the time they had thought the tiny mechanics were alien insects intent on devouring them rather than a harmless repair crew.

Tezoc's mercenaries were war-hardened soldiers, but Ryan had seen Carl's reaction to the swarm when he hadn't known they were harmless, and he was certain that the swarm would terrify even the bravest of men. All five mercs were now in the room. They must have felt so secure after Dan's capture they were no longer even guarding the door.

"On three," broadcast Ryan. He took a deep breath and gripped the globes a bit tighter. *"One. Two. Three!"*

They both stepped through the hole and lobbed their glass grenades in a high arc to different spots in the room. The instant their hands were free they removed the knives that were clamped between their teeth, ready to use them.

The four globes hit the floor one after another and exploded into fragments.

Reacting to the sudden sound of shattering glass around them, the mercs moved instantly, rolling away from the sound and coming up with their weapons at the ready. Finding no targets other than broken glass to shoot at, they scanned the room rapidly, their feet and their weapons shifting along with their eyes.

The soldier closest to the siblings saw them immediately and rushed forward so quickly he had them in his sights, at point-blank range, before they were able to blink.

Major Manning snapped his fingers and pointed at the opening in the wall. Two men lined up on either side of it and plunged through, rifle-first, and then separated, walking rapidly in different directions through the corridor, their weapons pointing ahead of them and their fingers on the triggers. They reappeared about thirty seconds later. "All clear," they reported.

Finally, the rapid-fire movements of the mercs stopped and the room became filled by an eerie silence.

One of the men crouched down and picked up a shard of glass, holding it up in front of his face and examining it carefully. He brought it to his nose and sniffed cautiously to determine if the globes had contained sleeping gas or any other substance that could prove dangerous. Detecting none, he looked up at his fellow soldiers and shook his head.

"Where did these kids come from?" demanded one of the soldiers. "How is it Tezoc didn't know they were here? He gave the all clear. Maybe his telepathic powers aren't what they're cracked up to be."

Ryan glanced over at the prisoners for the first time. They had recovered from their shock at the dramatic appearance of the team's two youngest members, and their eyes gleamed hopefully, all having guessed the kids' plan. While their mother had guessed their plan as well, a tear was slowly sliding down her face and Ryan knew she was terrified for her children. She would have far preferred they stay away and protect themselves rather than try to be heroes.

The soldier holding them at gunpoint motioned with his head for them to move into the center of the room. Although their hands were raised in surrender, neither had let go of their knives. Their captor started laughing and shook his head at Regan in disbelief. "A knife, little girl?" he said mockingly. "You two were going up against us with some glass balls and a few *knives?*" he continued. "You have to be kidding me."

"That is so cute," added another mercenary mockingly.

While four of the five men were laughing, one was decidedly not.

Major Manning maintained an expression that was deadly serious. Although short and thin, and still wearing a silly looking black ball-cap, Tezoc's second in command radiated more menace than all of the other men combined.

"These aren't just any kids, you idiots!" barked the major, his forceful voice cutting through the laughter like a knife. "These children are Ryan and Regan Resnick," he said icily. "And you would do well not to underestimate them."

The laughter stopped immediately. The mercs knew that both Tezoc and Manning had spent long hours studying all Prometheus personnel. These two must be on the team. The Prometheus Project had resorted to recruiting kids. How *pathetic*. But what was even more pathetic was how seriously Major Manning was taking them.

And then, right on cue, the nanobots appeared!

They shot from the floor like black lava from a volcanic eruption. They each had six identical body segments and looked far fiercer and more deadly than the most savage collection of army ants. As they crossed pieces of the globe, the glass melted away under their gnashing jaws and ever-moving pincers. They continued pouring from the floor; a ravenous, unstoppable black wave of destruction.

The soldiers began to panic at what they thought was a deadly threat more horrible than any they had ever faced. They were in the soldiering business and were fully prepared to die, but not by having their flesh picked clean from their bones in seconds by thousands and thousands of razor-sharp teeth.

Ryan and Regan had been ready for this moment. With the appearance of the nanobots their captors forgot about them entirely. Ryan slid across the floor, completely ignoring the tiny black machines, and stopped just behind Carl. Regan did the same, stopping behind Miguel. Using their knives, they immediately went to work on the prisoners' plasticuffs, sawing away at the hardened plastic with all of their strength.

The mercenaries fired wildly into the swarm with no effect. The relentless insect army just kept coming, melting away every piece of glass in its path. After a few seconds, the shooting stopped as each soldier realized it was hopeless. They couldn't possibly kill enough of these bugs to delay their advance for even an instant.

Panicked, the soldiers dropped their guns and began looking for an escape route.

Ryan continued to saw furiously through the plasticuffs around Carl's wrists. In seconds Carl's hands would be free, and while the intruders were panicked and distracted, Carl would have his choice of their abandoned weapons. While Regan wasn't as strong as her brother, she was making great progress freeing Miguel.

The plan was working perfectly! Ryan was certain their victory was assured.

But then again, Ryan couldn't have possibly predicted what was about to happen next.

CHAPTER 13

Plan B

The nanobots began retreating!

Impossible. This had never happened before.

But impossible or not, they began melting back into the floor with great speed, like oil pouring down a drain.

The mercenaries quickly regained their composure as the nanobot threat dissipated. In seconds the mercs had realized what the kids were up to and yanked them off the ground, effortlessly disarming them at the same time.

Two other mercs pulled zip-strips from their belts, and after two quick zipping sounds Carl and Miguel were bound as securely as they had been before the rescue attempt.

Ryan was furious! *How had this happened?*

When the nanobots knew damage was being done

for experimental purposes, as when his father had cut holes in the orange ceramic wall, they would not emerge and they would not repair further damage to the object. This is why they didn't repair the wall after Major Manning's rifle shot had shattered a portion of it. But once they emerged—as long as they weren't actively blocked from the object they were trying to repair—they had always finished the job. Why had they retreated halfway through? They had never done this before. Never! Ryan couldn't believe it. His plan had been seconds away from success.

Even more unusual, about ten of the tiny mechanics had stopped dead in their tracks in the middle of the floor. What was going on?

Major Manning walked slowly to the motionless nanobots and knelt down. He picked up one of the tiny robots, held it up, and examined it. He then turned in disgust to his fellow soldiers. *"You men are pathetic,"* he roared. "You call yourselves professionals! These things were just here to repair the globes, you idiots. Am I the only one who remembered Tezoc's briefing? Am I! Tezoc specifically warned us about this, remember? He told us that when something in the city is damaged it sends out a swarm of tiny robots to make repairs. Tezoc even told us they would look deadly but not to worry. Is this ringing a bell in any of your thick, worthless skulls?"

The expressions on the mercs' faces made it clear

that they did now remember and were embarrassed by their reaction.

"This was their plan all along," continued the major. "They counted on us all to panic while they went about freeing their people with those harmless knives you were laughing about," he said in disgust. "The ones you were sure posed absolutely no threat to us. We were just lucky the bug-things decided to retreat when they did or the kids' plan would have worked."

Manning removed a small container from his pocket and scooped up the immobile nanobots in front of him. "I'll show these to Tezoc later on," he said, slipping the container back into his pocket.

He rose and walked over to the two kids. "Nice try," he said sincerely. "You're as capable as the information we have about you would suggest. I wish my men here had *half* your brains and courage." He paused and leaned forward. "So tell me . . . how is it that Tezoc didn't sense you in the city?" he asked with great interest.

Ryan shrugged his shoulders. "I don't know," he lied. "Maybe he can only sense adults."

The major's eyebrows came together in thought for just a moment, but then he shook his head ever so slightly, dismissing Ryan's explanation. "Don't worry," he said, removing several black zip-strips to bind the newcomers and add them to his collection of prisoners. "I'm sure with a little experimentation, we'll figure it out in no time."

Ryan was quickly developing a headache to add to his other problems, but he forced himself to ignore the pain. They had developed a backup strategy in case their rescue attempt failed, and he wasn't about to let a headache distract him.

"Time for plan B," he broadcast to Regan.

"Let's do it," she replied.

Ryan gathered his thoughts and then met Manning's eyes confidently. "Before you cuff us, I have a deal to propose."

The short mercenary appeared amused. "A deal?"

Regan nodded beside her brother, forcing herself to look cool and confident as well.

Manning smiled without warmth. "For us to make a deal, you would need to have something we want. Since we already have everything we want, you might as well save your breath."

"Not everything," pointed out Ryan. "You want to get out of this city, don't you?"

"How do you know that?"

"We overheard Tezoc admit that the technology he brought with him to exit the city isn't working."

The major raised his eyebrows. "Go on," he said.

"Well, we think we've figured out where to find technology in this city that *can* nullify the force-field."

"Figured out?" said Manning in disbelief. "Just like that?" he said, snapping his fingers. "What are the odds that you figured this out right when you needed a bar-gaining chip?"

"Pretty good, actually," said Regan. "Since my dad already created an entrance, we never tried to figure it out before. When we overheard Tezoc, though, we thought about it very hard and put a lot of puzzle pieces together. We think we've almost solved it."

"That must have been some pretty remarkable reasoning."

"*You* were the one who said not to underestimate us," Regan reminded him. "Besides, you don't have to believe us. Let us go and we'll *prove* it. We'll bring the force-field nullifier back to you."

"I have a better idea. Why don't you tell me where it is?"

"Because we're not sure," said Ryan. "Yet. We still have to solve a few remaining pieces of the puzzle—but we're very, very close."

"So you want me to just let you go?" he said, amused. "Just like that?" He paused. "How do I know you'll even *try* to find what we want? How do I know you won't plan another rescue?"

"Because we believe Tezoc when he says he'll kill our mom if our dad can't find a way out in time," said Ryan. "That's why we started thinking about this in the first place. With our mother's life on the line, do you really think we won't do everything we can to find the technology and return it to Tezoc in time?"

Manning studied Ryan carefully but said nothing.

"We're also out of ideas for a rescue," he continued. "Two kids against armed, trained soldiers. We'd rather spend our time trying to save our mom."

"All we ask," added Regan, "is that if we do find a way out, you promise not to hurt anyone on the Prometheus team."

The major considered. "Okay," he said finally. "You have a deal. You make some good points. If your dad doesn't come through, perhaps you will at that." He motioned to a soldier with a long, thin face and thin lips. "But there is no way I'm letting you just go. You must think I'm an idiot. Lieutenant Davidenko here will accompany you."

The lieutenant stepped forward.

"Lieutenant, I want you to give them free reign and not slow them down. If they find anything, however, I want you to bring them back here immediately. You are not to bother Tezoc with it. I'll examine what they find and make sure it works and isn't a trick. Is that understood?"

"Yes, sir," said Davidenko.

Ryan and Regan turned to leave with their new escort following.

"Oh, and Lieutenant, one last thing. If they go anywhere near where Ben Resnick is working, or if they attempt to escape," said Manning with deadly conviction. "I want you to shoot them both without mercy."

CHAPTER 14

Escape Route

U nder the circumstances, they knew, they had done well. While they were still prisoners, at least they weren't bound and gagged on the floor of the invaders' headquarters. At least they had a chance to escape.

They had tried to think of a way out of the city to protect their mother from Tezoc's threat—tried to think of what a force-field nullifier would look like, or where one would be, but had gotten nowhere. At least their attempt had given them the idea for a bluff. Now all they had to do, with time quickly running out, was escape from a heavily armed mercenary without having any plan, find a way to rescue the prisoners—again without a plan—and then rescue their father and defeat all the deadly enemy soldiers.

Piece of cake, thought Ryan miserably as they exited the building.

"Where to?" snapped Davidenko angrily, annoyed that he had been chosen for a baby-sitting mission.

"We need to take a Hauler," said Ryan.

"A Hauler?"

Regan pointed to one of several of the green, electric trucks outside the building. "One of those," she explained. "We need you to drive."

Davidenko laughed. "Sure. Good idea. I suppose you'd be willing to hold my weapon for me."

Regan smiled innocently. "Okay," she said.

The lieutenant shook his head. "Your brother will drive."

"I can't," said Ryan. "I don't have my license. I'm allowed to drive a golf-cart but not a truck."

"Drive!" ordered Davidenko impatiently. "Are you seriously worried about breaking driving laws? I'd be more worried about saving my mother's life if I were you. Besides, I don't think we'll be running into any traffic cops," he added sarcastically.

Ryan got in the driver's side and Regan sat beside him. Davidenko stationed himself behind them with his machine gun trained on their backs.

Regan nodded slightly toward the assault rifle. "Do you have to point that at us?" she asked. "Do you think we'll be able to take it away from you if you don't?"

Davidenko smiled broadly. "Not in this lifetime."

"So what are you worried about?" pressed Regan. "If we make a run for it you'll still have plenty of time to shoot us. Or are you such a bad shot, you don't think you can hit us even with a gun like that?"

Davidenko didn't respond, but a few seconds later he lowered the rifle and put it in his lap. "Let's go," he instructed Ryan.

"*Any ideas?*" broadcast Regan.

"No," answered Ryan telepathically. "*You?*"

"*None.*"

"*I guess I'll just drive and pretend to know where I'm going until we figure something out.*" As he sent the message, Ryan started the Hauler and began to pull forward jerkily.

Ryan drove aimlessly around the city for five minutes. Thankfully for all involved, his herky-jerky driving got better he went along. No one spoke, although both kids were deep in thought the entire time.

"*Ryan,*" broadcast his sister, finally. "*What if we went to the zoo building? We could go to a planet with dangerous animals and try to lose him there. One where we know which animals are deadly and which aren't. It would give us the advantage.*"

Ryan nodded. "*Good thinking, Regs,*" he broadcast, abruptly changing direction. It was a long shot, but far better than any plan he had been able to come up with.

Once again, they drove for several minutes in silence, both of them trying to remember all the planets they had visited through the zoo's portals and which would provide the best chance of escaping the lieutenant.

Once more it was Regan who hit upon the answer. *"How about Walendam?"* she proposed. *"There are usually lots of furry rynows near the force-field. They'd do the trick."*

"Perfect," broadcast Ryan admiringly, feeling at least a tiny bit hopeful for the first time since they had begun driving.

Walendam was a planet whose animal life resembled the wildlife of Africa in many ways. They had watched one animal there, in particular, for many hours with their mother because it reminded them of a cross between a rhino and a cow. A rynow.

On Earth, the rhinoceros had terrible eyesight, but was very fast and was good at detecting movement. If a rhino charged and you ran, you were in big trouble. If you stood perfectly still, however, the animal could easily lose sight of you and wander off. The rynow was very similar in this respect, both in terms of its eyesight and its dangerous horn. The features that made it different from a rhino, however, were perfect for their needs. First, it was covered in fluffy black fur, like a dog, and was somewhat cow-like in appearance. It might have looked soft to predators, but underneath its fur it had body armor like a tank. Its nasty horn was retractable and could only be seen when it was about to charge. This made the animal appear very harmless—almost cuddly even. Davidenko wouldn't think it was dangerous until it was too late.

All they had to do was step through a zoo portal to Walendam, telling Davidenko they were looking for an important clue. They would then take a tram and drive it through the force-field barrier surrounding the entry point and right into a rynow ambush. The mercenary wouldn't have any idea he was in danger. They would stay totally still while Davidenko, knowing nothing about these animals, moved and made himself their target.

The plan was far from foolproof. They would have to be lucky for it to succeed—very lucky. On the other hand, while being closely guarded by a trigger-happy mercenary, any plan that gave them even a small chance of success was a good one.

Ryan glanced at his watch as they turned a corner and the zoo came into view in the distance, along with their parents' octagonal lab building. If this was going to work—and Ryan knew the odds were against them— it had better work quickly. About four hours had passed since Tezoc had made his deadly threat. Which meant they only had two hours left.

He looked longingly at his parents' building. Had it really only been five hours earlier when they had awakened there. It seemed like days had gone by since then.

Ryan barely managed not to gasp as a sudden flash of inspiration surged through him like electricity. His parents' lab building! *That* was the key. But he needed to work out a detailed plan. His mind raced, and in less than a minute he had it! The corners of his mouth turned up into the slightest of smiles.

Regan's plan to ambush Davidenko on Walendam had been good. But his was better.

And with just a fraction of the luck they would have needed on Walendam—and some good performances— they might just be free of Davidenko.

They might be free of him far sooner than they had imagined.

CHAPTER 15

Escape

"Regan, I need you to pretend to get sick to your stomach."

"Why?" she broadcast back.

"No time. You'll see. Just do it."

"Are you sure you know what you're doing?"

"You'll have to trust me," he replied adamantly. "Hurry."

Regan moaned loudly. "I feel horrible," she complained.

"Tell me to stop the truck," broadcast Ryan.

"Stop the truck, Ryan," said Regan aloud. "I think . . . I might have to . . . vomit."

Ryan stopped the Hauler abruptly and everyone got out. Regan stumbled away from the truck and dropped to the ground, rolling onto her back and groaning.

"Good acting," sent Ryan. Another of her performances flashed into his mind for just a moment, when her pretend vomiting had created the diversion they had needed to enter the city for the very first time.

"There's a nasty flu going around school," explained Ryan as Davidenko looked on. "She must have caught it."

Ryan reached into his pocket and—

"Freeze!" barked the lieutenant, his rifle up instantly.

"Okay, okay, okay," said Ryan nervously. "Take it easy. I'm just trying to help my sister. Don't shoot."

Ryan pulled his hand from his pocket very, very slowly and removed what looked like a fancy, expensive pen. He opened his hand, allowing Davidenko to examine it while it sat in his palm.

"What is it?"

"It's an alien medical kit," answered Ryan.

Regan continued to make soft groaning sounds on the ground next to him and did a convincing job of looking nauseous.

"Watch," said Ryan. He pointed the device at his sister. As he moved the device it changed colors so that it always stood out from its surroundings. As he pressed the bottom button the small triangle at the tip of the device glowed briefly and then stopped.

"Okay," Ryan instructed his sister telepathically, *"have an instant recovery now."*

Regan had no idea what Ryan was up to, but at this

point she had no choice but to do as he asked and hope for the best. She waited a few seconds and then breathed a heavy sigh of relief. "Thanks, Ryan. I feel much better." She hopped to her feet. "Okay, let's go."

Davidenko shook his head and sneered. "You two think I was born yesterday, don't you? That was just an act. That isn't a magical medical pen, you were just pretending for some reason. Why?"

"Not an act," said Ryan. "When you push the bottom button it attacks infections. It must have already killed off all the viruses causing my sister's flu. The top button helps wounds heal faster, and the middle one will give you complete pain relief for about thirty minutes." Ryan paused. "I'll show you," he offered, turning the pen toward Davidenko.

"Push that button and you're dead," barked the lieutenant.

Ryan shook his head. "Not very trusting, are you? Suppose for a moment this isn't a weapon and I'm not trying to trick you. Suppose it really does what I say. If you could learn how it works, how much would medical technology like that be worth?"

Davidenko smiled slowly. "Billions and billions," he said simply.

Ryan began to slip the device into his pocket once again.

"Not so fast," said the lieutenant. "I think I *would*

like a demonstration, after all. First, point it at your sister and press the other two buttons. I want to make sure nothing happens to her."

"Still no time to explain?" asked a confused Regan.

"I'm afraid not. But don't worry, you'll catch on."

Ryan pointed the device at Regan and pressed the top button. The tip of the device glowed. He pressed the middle button and it glowed again. Ryan glanced up at their captor. "Satisfied?" he asked.

Davidenko nodded and considered what he should do next.

"Wow, Ryan, that pain setting really works," broadcast Regan. *"The nasty headache I got when we were talking to Manning went away the second you pressed the button."*

"Okay," said Davidenko, having made up his mind. "Let's do this. Try it out on me."

"But you aren't sick or wounded," pointed out Ryan. "Are you in any pain?"

The merc shook his head, no.

"Then how will you know it works?"

Davidenko considered this, frowning. "Good question," he said finally. "I don't know." He noticed an amused look on Ryan's face. "Let me guess," he snapped. "You have an idea?"

"As a matter of fact," said Ryan happily, "I do. My idea is to kick you—hard—in the leg. Then I can use the pain setting and you'll know if it works or not."

The mercenary thought about this. "Go ahead," he said. "But let me warn you. If your pen doesn't work, I'm going to kick you back. Hard."

"Don't worry," said Ryan. "It'll work."

Ryan pulled his foot back and kicked Davidenko in the shin as hard as he could. The merc cursed several times through clenched teeth.

"Can you feel any pain now?" asked Ryan innocently, fighting back a smile.

"Quit stalling and use the pen!" demanded Davidenko.

Ryan pointed the alien medical device at the mercenary and pressed the middle button. The tip glowed softly once again.

Davidenko's eyes widened in surprise and delight. "You were right," he said in disbelief. "That's amazing. My leg stopped hurting immediately."

"Told you," said Ryan, slipping the device into his pocket.

"I'll take that now," said Davidenko predictably.

Ryan frowned and handed the device over to him. "Okay," he said. "But we really need to get moving. My sister and I are convinced that the last clue is in this building." He pointed to their parents' lab.

"*I hope you know what you're doing, Ryan,*" broadcast his sister.

"*Yeah. Me too,*" he responded wryly.

They led the lieutenant to one of the invisible doors,

a section of the silver wall that promptly vanished and then reappeared behind them after they entered. The mercenary was clearly surprised by this, looking back to where the doorway had appeared with a puzzled look on his face, but remained silent.

Ryan pointed to a washing-machine sized object at the side of the stainless-steel table in the middle of the room. "That," he said, "is a holographic projector. I'm pretty sure it'll give us the final clue. We need you to go over there and flip the switch in the middle."

"What will it do?" said the mercenary suspiciously. "And why me? Why don't you do it?"

"It will project a holographic map of the city covered with strange symbols. We think we can decipher them and find a force-field nullifier."

"Again," pressed Davidenko, "why don't you flip the switch?"

Ryan appeared nervous. "We, ah . . . we could. I mean, there is no reason we *couldn't*. But you have to be standing at this exact spot to read the clue, and it only stays on for a few seconds, so we ah . . . we need to be standing here."

"Is that so?"

Regan's eyes widened as she finally realized what her brother's plan must be. "Ah . . . absolutely," she responded, using her own acting talents to assist her brother. "That device is completely harmless," she assured Davidenko, knowing that this would only make him more suspicious. "Just turn it on and we'll read the clue from right here. Then we'll be able to find the technology Tezoc needs to exit the city. Everyone will be happy."

"I have a better idea," insisted Davidenko. "You two go over there and turn it on. I'll stand here and watch for the hologram."

"But . . . but you won't know what to look for," stammered Ryan.

Davidenko smiled. "We can always do it again. But you have to try it first. Just like with the pen. I'm not about to walk into one of your traps."

"What are you talking about," complained Ryan. "I told you the truth about the alien medical device. Why can't you trust us?"

The mercenary laughed. "That's how I've managed to stay alive for this long. By not letting myself get out-smarted by the likes of you." The lieutenant smiled, very pleased with himself. "Now move!" he barked.

The siblings walked dejectedly to the generator.

Davidenko raised his weapon and pointed it at them. "Okay, no funny business. If I get the slightest hint you're trying to trick me, I'll shoot first and ask questions later."

They nodded. Ryan stared calmly at the lieutenant and then reached forward and flipped the switch.

Nothing happened.

Five seconds passed.

"What's wrong?" said Davidenko, his weapon still raised and his finger placed squarely on the trigger.

Ryan shook his head. "Nothing. It takes about fifteen seconds to warm up. You'll see the hologram any second."

"I had better," said Davidenko. "Because if this is some kind of stu—"

He never finished his sentence. In mid-word he collapsed to the ground like a sack of cement.

"Yesssss!" said Ryan excitedly. He flipped the switch the other way, turning the ultrasonic generator off, and then hugged his sister in elation.

They had done it! They were free from Davidenko. His plan had worked perfectly!

They both rushed up to the fallen mercenary and Ryan checked for a pulse.

"Well?" said his sister worriedly.

"It's weak, but he's alive."

Regan blew out a relieved breath. They needed to escape, but they certainly didn't want to be responsible for *killing* someone—not even a merc who wouldn't have hesitated to do the same to them.

"He'll probably make a full recovery," continued Ryan. "But I'm guessing it'll take a long while."

Regan nodded. "Now *that* was a great plan, Ryan," she said in admiration.

"Thanks," he said with a wide grin. "I guess I was lucky everything fell into place," he added, trying to be modest.

"Luck had nothing to do with it," said Regan. "You couldn't have played that any better."

Ryan couldn't help but smile proudly. He had expected it to be fairly simple to trick the mercenary into standing exactly where he and Regan had stood when *they* were blasted by the ultrasonic generator. He knew if they appeared desperate to be standing there when the machine was turned on, the suspicious Davidenko would *demand* to take up this position himself. The hard part had been tricking him into letting Ryan strip him of his ability to feel pain. If not for this, the instant they turned on the ultrasonic generator he would have shot them both and fled the building, screaming in agony, just as he and his sister had done. Luckily for them, they had felt the crushing, blinding pain the generator had caused immediately—not that it had seemed so lucky at the time.

"That alien medical device is *amazing*," said Ryan. "*Beyond* amazing. The ultrasonic energy must have been practically vibrating his skull off and he didn't feel a *thing*. He had absolutely *no idea* he was being attacked up until the time he passed out."

"I guess pain really does have its purposes," said Regan, beaming happily. "You'll have to be sure to tell your teacher all about it if we ever get out of this."

Her brother smiled. "Do you think that's why she taught it—so her students could use this knowledge to knock out machine gun carrying mercenaries?"

"Of course," said Regan, grinning. "What other reason could there be?"

Ryan paused. "Well, we've accomplished the first part of the plan," he noted. "We're free again. But we have less than two hours to free the rest of the team and save Mom and Dad. Our chances were one in a billion. Now, I'd guess they've improved to one in a million."

"I don't know, Ryan," said his sister, her eyes twinkling. "They might just be a lot better than you think."

"Why do you say that?"

"Because while we were driving, I think I really did figure out where to find a force-field nullifier. If we're lucky, we might just have a bargaining chip after all."

Harris County Public Library
HCPL LaPorte
05/11/12 03:21PM

To renew call: 713-747-4763
or visit: www.hcpl.net
You must have your library card number
and pin number to renew.

PATRON: MILLER RICKY ANTHONY

Captured /
CALL NO: Richar SF
 3402807736856B
DUE: 05/25/12

TOTAL: 1

CHAPTER 16

The Force-Field Nullifier

"**F**antastic," said Ryan. "But let's take care of Davidenko before you tell me about it," he advised. "I doubt he'll be waking up anytime soon, but let's not take chances."

Together they rolled the lieutenant onto his stomach and pulled his arms behind him. While Ryan held his wrists and then his ankles together, Regan bound them tightly with zip-strips they had removed from his belt.

They decided not to take Davidenko's assault rifle. Neither of them knew how to use it. If they tried, the weapon could easily prove to be more dangerous to them than to their enemies.

They removed Davidenko's belt, stuffed with spare clips and an assortment of other gear. Regan quickly began examining the contents of the bulging black pouches clipped onto the belt while her brother searched the mercenary's pockets and body. Ryan found a combat knife in a black-leather sheath strapped to the side of the soldier's lower leg and removed it for possible future use. He also found the medical device Davidenko had taken from him and replaced it in his own pocket where it belonged.

Regan removed two small cylindrical tubes from a belt pouch. They resembled soda cans with clips protruding from their tops. She handed one to her brother. "Flashbangs," she noted unnecessarily.

Ryan took one and nodded. These might be just what they needed for their next rescue attempt. Not only had they learned science from some of the greatest scientists of the day, Colonel Carl Sharp had taught them a thing or two about military equipment.

Stun grenades, also called flashbangs, were first used by the military in hostage rescue situations and were ideal for this purpose. These canisters were packed with a mixture of aluminum and potassium perchlorate—also known as flashpowder. Flashpowder was originally used in early flash cameras and by magicians, and was still used in fireworks and to create special effects for movies. This powder burnt very brightly and so quickly it seemed to "flash" out of existence. Flashbang grenades were not designed to cause any permanent damage, but like their name implied, simply to cause such an intensely bright flash and earsplitting bang that they would blind and deafen an enemy for about ten seconds.

While the rifle was of no use to the siblings, the knife and flashbangs might come in very handy.

Ryan found nothing else of interest, while Regan found only one additional useful item: a small stun gun that she slipped into her pocket. When fired, two small electrodes still attached by wires to the device would shoot out like dual harpoons. They would release an electrical charge capable of overloading the body's electrical communication system, causing confusion and paralyzing muscles but not doing any permanent damage.

With Davidenko bound and their thorough inspection of his gear completed, Ryan was eager to hear what his sister had discovered.

Regan was confident of her logic, but she knew it wouldn't be easy to convince her brother. She decided to get to the point fairly quickly and then go from there. She took a deep breath. "As we drove toward the zoo building," she began, "I was thinking through the details of the rynow plan. How would we convince Davidenko to go through the portal to Walendam? How would we convince him to let us drive him in a tram once we arrived? That sort of thing."

Ryan nodded. He had been doing the same thing.

"Davidenko would let us go anywhere we wanted, as long as he still thought we were trying to help his boss get through the force-field. So it was obvious that we just had to convince him that we were going to Walendam and taking a tram through the barrier to find a force-field nullifier. In case he didn't believe us, I began thinking of arguments that would support our lie. And then I realized something," she continued, shaking her head in wonder. "It *wasn't* a lie. The trams on the zoo planets really are the answer. They each have nullifiers we can use to get through the Prometheus shield."

Ryan shook his head and reacted exactly as she had known he would. "Dad already considered this and ruled it out," he said, unable to completely hide his disappointment.

"Yes, but he's never tested it," pointed out Regan. "The more I thought through the arguments the more convinced I became that Dad is wrong," she said bluntly. "I'm almost sure of it."

Ryan raised his eyebrows. "In what way?" he said.

"We know the planets all have force-field barriers to protect visitors, and we know when you're in a tram you can just drive right through them if you want to explore."

Ryan nodded. "Right. That's why Dad considered the idea in the first place."

"But he didn't consider it carefully enough. He measured the frequencies of the shields on each planet and found they were all different. Different from each other and different from the Prometheus shield. Because of this he figured that even if there was some device on the tram—like an alien garage-door opener—used to cross a barrier on a given planet, it wouldn't work here. He knew from his own work that only something with the exact opposite frequency from that of the force-field could create an opening. Just like our garage-door remote on Earth—it can't open anyone else's door."

Regan paused to see if her brother had any questions.

"Go on," he said.

"Also, while some planets have more trams than others, and they come in a variety of sizes, they all work the same way and have the same design. Dad was convinced the Qwervy wouldn't go to all the trouble of having different nullifiers for every different planet. He figured it would be far simpler for them to engineer the force-field barriers *themselves* to detect trams and let them pass. When a tram approached, the barrier would detect it and create a hole in itself for a second to let it through. The technology for this would be in the force-field, not the tram. He was so sure of his reasoning, and so busy, he never took the time to test it—besides, he had already created an opening in the Prometheus shield that was working really well."

Ryan frowned. "He never did test his hypothesis, I'll give you that. And he's the one always saying how important that is. He says scientists can't make assumptions. They need to test every hypothesis, even the ones they think are obvious."

"Exactly," said Regan. "That's all I'm asking. That we test it. Because I'm convinced he's wrong. I've thought about it a totally different way and come up with a totally different answer. Let me ask you this: why is there a force-field barrier around this city in the first place?"

"To protect it," replied Ryan.

"From what?"

"From us."

Regan shook her head. "Isn't the shield really there to protect *us*? *From the city?* The Qwervy wanted to be absolutely certain we primitives wouldn't get in and accidentally hurt ourselves. Just like locking a gun away from a bunch of kids protects *them*."

Ryan nodded. She was right, of course.

"Dad thinks of the field as a two-way barrier," she continued. "Made to be very difficult to open in *either* direction. And no one knows better than Dad how remarkable the barrier really is. He admits that it practically took a miracle for him to discover a way to break through it." She paused. "But the city is off limits to all but a few authorized observers selected from the Qwervy and a few other advanced species. Wouldn't they make it easy for *themselves* to exit? They'd make it nearly impossible to *enter*—to keep us out—but someone already inside should be able to get out, easily, anytime they wanted," she insisted. "Maybe they would need to have a small device, or need to know a code, or maybe they would just have to ask the Teacher to create an exit telepathically."

Ryan considered. He had never thought about it this way, but Regan was making perfect sense.

"One of the reasons Dr Harris agreed to let us be part of the Prometheus Project," she continued, "is because kids aren't afraid to consider ideas adults have been taught to think are crazy or impossible. All of Dad's instincts and training tell him that the barrier is supposed to be just as difficult to exit as to enter. And human science could never build a tram garage-door opener that could work on thousands of force-field barriers, all with different frequencies. Human science was barely able to find a way through a single one, and even that took more equipment than could fit inside *three* trams. But so what?" she demanded. "Surely the Qwervy could pull it off. Just because Dad thinks it's impossible, doesn't mean the Qwervy can't do it."

She had a point there, Ryan had to admit. The Qwervy seemed to have a habit of doing the impossible. So why not? As he gazed at the fiery resolve in his sister's green eyes, he knew he had to give her the benefit of the doubt. If he had learned anything during the past several months it was to trust his sister's instincts.

He agreed to work with her to try to locate a nullifier, but only for thirty minutes or so. If they couldn't find one in that period of time they would need to abandon their efforts and make another attempt to rescue the prisoners.

They hurried to the zoo and rushed through a portal. They found themselves on a planet with three visible moons. In its reddish sky floated balloon-like animals the size of whales. Resembling massive jellyfish in the sky, they drifted through dense swarms of gnat-like insects, miles and miles across, sucking up many millions of the tiny creatures as they passed, like living vacuum cleaners. The two visitors forced themselves to turn away from this remarkable spectacle. There was no time for sightseeing.

The siblings quickly found a tram and activated its holographic display. They examined every hologram in front of them for several minutes but couldn't find anything that pointed them in the right direction.

"Time for plan B," said Ryan, holding up the hammer he had brought with him. "You know what the scientists have told us: sometimes, the best way to learn what something does is to take it apart."

"I think they meant taking it apart very gently and carefully, step by step," quipped Regan with a grin. "Not bashing it to pieces with a hammer."

Ryan shrugged his shoulders. "We're in a hurry," he said innocently. "Besides," he added playfully, "I'm pretty sure all of humanity's greatest scientific discoveries were made using a hammer."

With that they began their experiment. They drove the tram to the edge of the force-field and Ryan demolished pieces of it, one at a time. After each piece was smashed, they would quickly determine if the tram could still drive through the barrier. If so, they would back it up, smash another piece, and try again.

After twenty minutes of this, Ryan smashed one of the last pieces remaining on the inside of the tram, a light-red crystal medallion extending down like a circular rear-view mirror.

Regan moved the tram forward.

It slammed into the barrier and stopped!

Regan tried again. Again, the barrier remained firmly intact.

Ryan's eyes widened. Destroying the reddish crystal medallion destroyed the ability of the tram to get through the barrier. It was as simple as that.

Now full of excitement, they dashed back through the portal to the zoo and then on to another planet with a fully intact tram. They quickly spotted the same light-red crystal. This time, instead of destroying it, they worked to carefully remove it fully intact.

After only a few minutes it was free. Regan placed it in her pocket. She jumped from the tram and nodded to her brother.

Ryan moved the tram forward.

And it was stopped by the barrier!

Remarkable.

Regan approached the barrier with the crystal in her pocket. She took a step forward and walked right through the field.

It worked! There *was* a garage-door opener, and they had found it.

She had been right! The mechanism for lowering the barrier was in the tram rather than being in the barrier. They had found a nullifier. But the big question was, would it work on all the force-fields or only this particular one?

They returned to the zoo and hastily stepped through another portal to a different planet—this one covered with massive volcanoes—and a different barrier.

Regan approached the edge of the force-field with the medallion in her pocket. She took a deep breath and raised her foot to march forward. Would the medallion be able to nullify this field—one with a different frequency than the field it had just nullified?

There was only one way to find out.

"Cross your fingers, Ryan," she said nervously, knowing that their fate might very well depend on what happened between her last footfall and her next.

CHAPTER 17

A Thorny Puzzle

Regan completed her stride, unhindered.

The barrier melted away before the medallion in her pocket.

"Unbelievable," said Ryan. "Congratulations Regs. You know what this means, don't you?"

Regan nodded. "It means we have our bargaining chip."

"No," he said, grinning. "It means Dad was *wrong*. *About something scientific*. That doesn't happen every day."

Regan laughed, even though they both knew that their father would be more proud of her than anyone for having proven him wrong.

Ryan glanced at his watch. "It's been over five hours since Tezoc made his threat," he reported. "We'd better go."

They left the zoo and headed back toward the invaders' headquarters in the Hauler with Ryan at the wheel. Even though they had been bluffing at the time, they had made the deal with Manning to try to find the nullifier, so they would return to him. Besides, they couldn't be sure that Manning had even mentioned them to Tezoc. For all they knew, Tezoc would shoot them on sight if they went to where their father was working.

"Ryan," said Regan worriedly after they had started out. "Finding the nullifier makes me nervous. I think we've been missing something about Tezoc. Something is wrong. I can feel it. Something huge."

"Why do you say that?"

"Because it doesn't make sense that he wouldn't know how to exit this city," she replied. "I was right— there *are* fairly simple ways to exit. We found one. And I bet there are many others. Tezoc is just too smart, too good a planner, to have brought the wrong technology with him. He knows this city inside and out. And while his people aren't as advanced as the Qwervy, they're more advanced than we are. He was smart enough to break out of a prison no other of his kind had ever broken out of, but his entire plan might fail because he brought the wrong key with him?" She paused. "I just don't believe that," she finished emphatically.

Ryan thought about this and frowned. "So then what's going on? What could he gain by pretending not to be able to leave here? Why threaten Dad?"

"We're missing something important," insisted Regan.

"Maybe we should back up and try to think about this from the very beginning."

"Well, Tezoc captured Mom and Dad, and they said they wouldn't be back in the city until about six this morning. So the invasion probably happened around then," she said confidently.

Ryan nodded. "You're right. But I wanted to go all the way back to last Friday, when we got the telepathic warning about an unauthorized entry. Eight days ago. Tezoc must have been the cause. I'll bet that's when he first arrived."

Regan considered. They hadn't thought about this for a while. "And also exactly when we stopped being able to feel the Teacher," she reminded her brother.

"That's right," said Ryan, his eyes widening. For a week now they had been thinking the warning was a false alarm, after all. But it clearly was not. They needed to adjust their thinking. "So we were wrong: the warning wasn't a malfunction due to the Teacher leaving. The Teacher must still have been here when Tezoc came through."

"So did it decide to leave after it detected him?"

"I don't believe that. It would have known Tezoc wasn't authorized to be here. It would have tried to stop him. It wouldn't just leave us at his mercy."

"Given the timing, Ryan, there are only two possibilities. Either the computer left at almost the exact time Tezoc arrived, or—"

Ryan knew where his sister was heading and didn't like it. "Or Tezoc must have deactivated it," he said, finishing the sentence for her.

She nodded.

Ryan shook his head. "Deactivated the Teacher?" he said in disbelief. "Impossible. Not if it didn't want to be."

"Ryan, if the Teacher didn't leave—and you're sure it wouldn't do that—it's the only explanation that makes sense," she insisted. "Tezoc escapes prison on his planet and comes through the portal to Earth. The city begins to send out its warning, but Tezoc cuts it off in mid-sentence. At the same time he deactivates the central computer so it can't stop him."

"As much as I hate to believe it, that's probably what happened," said Ryan miserably. "Which means I'm starting to think you're right again: something very, very fishy is going on. Because if Tezoc knows enough about this city to turn off the central computer, it's hard to believe he wouldn't know how to get through the force-field."

Regan nodded, glad that her brother had come over to her way of thinking.

"But let's keep going," suggested Ryan. "So eight days ago he arrives and deactivates the computer. Then what happens?"

Regan considered. "Well, he was good, but not perfect. A few seconds of the city's telepathic warning did get sent. To us. So we got nervous and asked Carl to do a security sweep to look for an alien intruder."

"Yeah, that went really well," said Ryan, rolling his eyes. "Security did a sweep, all right. But they found nothing. Tezoc should have registered on their equipment."

"But that's not so surprising. Tezoc would've been prepared for this possibility. He probably has some technology that makes him invisible to our sensors."

Ryan nodded. His sister was probably right.

"So he arrives and doesn't get caught during the security sweep," she continued. "How does he recruit the mercenaries?"

"Good question," said Ryan. "And how does he do it so quickly? And why? What's the rush? He must have really been moving to set everything up in a week. He would have had to leave the city right away and start recruiting. He would have had to know exactly where to go to find mercs, and he would have had to convince them he could pay them the money he was promising."

"But how does he even get out in the first place?" asked Regan. "He has to get out of the city, and then the cavern, and then the Proact installation. It seems to me it would be almost as hard getting to the outside through security as it would be getting in. Almost. For starters, to even *get* aboveground, he would have to take the

Prometheus elevator. It's the only way. And it's guarded every second of every day."

"Okay," said Ryan. "So this guy breaks out of an unbreakable prison, defeats Qwervy portal security, deactivates the Teacher, and finds a way out of here. Then all he has to do is recruit his mercenary army almost instantly and plan a way to break back into the city. Another impossibility." Ryan frowned. "Maybe we're still sleeping and this is a dream, because I don't care if this guy is Superman and Houdini combined, he couldn't have pulled this off."

"The only problem is that he did," said Regan. She paused in thought and a troubled frown came over her face. "What if he had Carl's help?"

"What are you saying?"

"Look, Ryan, you know how much I like Carl. I'm not accusing him of anything. I'm just trying to explore every last possibility. Could Carl have done it?"

"Probably," answered Ryan. "He's the only one on Earth who could. He knows all the security schedules—he sets them—and he knows all of the bypasses and codes and passwords and backup systems. Carl *is* Prometheus security."

"Carl lost his memory the day of the sweep," she pointed out. "We thought he must have experimented with the chemical formula his Proact team had developed. But what if we were wrong. *What if he did find*

Tezoc that day? What if he helped him escape, and it was *Tezoc* who erased his memory?"

Ryan's breath stuck in his throat. He had forgotten! Carl *had* lost his memory.

"I can't believe that," he said finally, shaking his head. "No money or threat in the world could get Carl to help Tezoc. He wouldn't help him even if his life were on the line. I'm positive of it. And he's a prisoner just like the rest of the team." He paused. "Carl's face looked fairly calm, but did you see his eyes when Tezoc was bragging about taking over the city? They were blazing with fury. There must be another answer," he insisted. "Let's keep going."

Regan paused for several long seconds, considering. Ryan was right. She had seen Carl's eyes and his rage was unmistakable. He knew better than anyone what could happen if the technology of the city got into the wrong hands. She knew with absolute certainty that Carl would have been willing to sacrifice himself and the entire team to prevent that. She nodded her agreement. "Okay," she said finally.

Regan paused for a moment to remember where they had left off. "So Tezoc arrives, shuts down the computer, escapes, recruits his army, and breaks back in. Then what does he do?"

Ryan considered. "He shuts down our opening in the force-field and somehow knocks out everyone in the city."

"How does he do that?"

"Well, you heard Carl," said Ryan. "He didn't think it was gas. Could've been anything. Some device he brought. It could've been ultrasonic energy for all we know."

"And why did he close our one opening in the force-field and trap himself inside?"

"He told Carl he did it because he knew outside security would discover we'd been invaded and send the army after him. He said he trapped himself by accident because the technology he brought to exit somewhere else didn't work."

Regan shook her head. "Do you believe that? Wouldn't he test his device first to make sure it worked before he closed the only opening in the shield?"

"Yeah," said Ryan unhappily. "He would. It would be really dumb not to, and he isn't dumb."

"Exactly. So why was his next step to get Dad to create an exit? Why do that if he could easily leave anytime he wanted? And why the hurry? Why six hours?"

"The same questions we started with," said Ryan in frustration. "This hasn't gotten us anywhere."

The both sighed. It seemed hopeless. They were more certain than ever they were missing the big picture. But while they had raised a number of good questions they had not come up with a single good answer.

And discussion time was over. They had arrived at their destination and there was no time to waste.

They both took a deep breath and prepared to enter the building that contained Major Manning and three other enemy soldiers. They paused for a moment to steady their nerves, but only for a moment. There was no turning back now. And Tezoc's deadline expired in thirty minutes.

It was time to trade the force-field nullifier for their mother's life.

Chapter 18

Deadly Orders

Just as they were about to enter the building, Ryan spotted a Hauler off in the distance, moving away from them. He pointed it out to his sister. It was just a bit too far away for them to make out who was inside.

"Where is it headed?" asked Ryan telepathically.

Regan shrugged her shoulders. *"I don't know. It's going in the direction of the cavern. Dad and Tezoc are in the opposite direction,"* she noted.

Ryan frowned. Where could it be going? And why? Nothing was making sense. But he was determined to find the key to this puzzle. There had to be one. And once he found it, everything would fall into place and suddenly make *perfect* sense. He glanced at his watch and didn't like what he saw. If he was going to solve this puzzle, he had better do it soon.

"Ryan, we're being idiots," broadcast Regan. *"What are we thinking?"*

Ryan gave her a puzzled look.

"We're both about to go in here together," she explained. *"One of us should stay outside in case something goes wrong. So we have a plan B."*

She was right! They *were* being idiots.

Ryan's eyes went wide as he realized the possibilities. The mercs didn't know they had escaped Davidenko. This made some excellent backup strategies possible. His sister had just significantly improved their chances of success. *"Regan, you're a genius."*

"Thanks. Another way to look at it is that I'm a chicken, but I like the way you're looking at it better."

Ryan smiled. *"I know exactly how to play this. Wait by the entrance here out of sight."*

"Should I sneak around back to the hallway?"

Ryan shook his head. *"No. Stay close to the main entrance."*

The mercenaries might be nothing but cold-blooded criminals, but they were very highly trained cold-blooded criminals. And they had been surprised twice from the corridor, once when the siblings had hidden with Dan, and once when they had tried to rescue the prisoners using the glass globes. Surely the mercs would have searched the corridor to learn how members of the Prometheus team had managed to magically appear twice in this location. Even if they hadn't found the invisible door, they would have rigged a booby-trap or some sort of warning so they wouldn't be surprised this way a third time.

Ryan handed his sister the combat knife he had taken from Davidenko to keep while he was inside.

"Good luck, Ryan," she broadcast worriedly.

Ryan shook his head. *"I won't need luck,"* he replied confidently. *"Not when I have you backing me up."*

Regan managed a nervous smile, wishing she had as much confidence in her ambushing skills as he seemed to have. She made her way to the corner of the building nearest the entrance, crouching low to stay out of sight.

Ryan walked the last few yards to the entrance. He raised his hands above his head and slowly walked through.

He scanned the room as he entered. There was only a single mercenary inside and now only one group of prisoners. Carl and his security team were gone! The one mercenary remaining had his rifle up and trained on Ryan by the time Ryan had completed his second step.

His hands still raised in surrender, Ryan walked forward toward the middle of the room and the lone mercenary. He examined the prisoners carefully. All of the scientists were where they had been before. Except one.

He stifled a gasp. His mom was missing! *Where was she!*

"Okay in there?" broadcast Regan.

Ryan forced himself to remain focused. *"Fine,"* he replied telepathically. *"Only one merc,"* he continued rapidly. *"The Prometheus security team and Mom aren't here. Neither is Manning."*

The soldier looked Ryan over carefully, a cruel scowl on his face. As Ryan stared into his eyes he became convinced that this man wasn't in the mercenary business for the money—this man just liked to hurt people. Ryan realized that this was the soldier Tezoc had referred to as Captain Brice, the man who had earlier threatened to shoot Carl in the leg.

Ryan remembered that Tezoc had gone ballistic over that. Why? Why had Tezoc threatened death to anyone who as much as scratched Carl? Why would he care? Tezoc didn't seem to care about the condition of any of the other prisoners. Ryan had a feeling that this was another piece of the puzzle—an important piece—but he didn't have time to consider it right now.

"Where is your sister?" demanded the soldier.

"Where do you think?" replied Ryan defiantly. "She's with Davidenko."

"How did you escape?"

"I didn't. We figured out where the nullifier technology is. Davidenko's going with Regan to get it. He sent me here to report."

Brice scowled. "And why should I believe you?"

"You're right," said Ryan, rolling his eyes. "I'm lying to you. Actually we knocked Davidenko unconscious and have him handcuffed in a building somewhere."

Brice smiled. "Very funny," he said. "So how long until Davidenko and your sister return?"

"They'll be here soon," said Ryan.

"So what do you have to report?"

"Where is my mother?" asked Ryan anxiously.

"Ah, yes, your mother," taunted Brice cheerfully. "She was moved. Tezoc wanted to make sure your father didn't slow down, so he brought her to where your father is working to, ah . . . motivate him."

"And the Prometheus security team?"

"What is this!" barked Brice angrily. "An interrogation? No more questions! It's time for you to answer mine. What have you come here to say?"

Ryan shook his head. "We made our deal with Major Manning. Where is he?"

Brice laughed. "So you prefer your friend Major Manning, do you? Well, he's not here right now." He leaned closer and whispered, "But I'll let you in on a little secret. He left orders for me to kill you both if you returned."

Ryan shrank back in horror. "You're lying."

Brice laughed even harder. "Guess again," he said. "And as soon as Davidenko gets back here with your sister, I intend to carry out my orders."

Ryan had recovered from the shock and his mind began working overtime. "But that doesn't make any sense. We had a deal. The nullifier for my mother's life and the safety of the Prometheus team. We're harmless and we're trying to help Tezoc find a way to exit the city." Ryan paused. "Does Tezoc even know about this?" he demanded.

"Manning said he spoke with him about it. I don't know for sure. What I do know is that Tezoc left clear instructions to follow the major's orders while he was busy at the other site."

"Call Tezoc, then. Check on the orders."

"I'm not going to bother Tezoc," said Brice. "Besides," he continued, the corners of his mouth turning up into a malevolent smile. "What if he says not to kill you? Then what would I do for fun?"

Ryan ignored the soldier's cruel taunt. "Why would Tezoc order us killed?" he pressed. "Doesn't that bother you? There's no guarantee my father can get us out of here. Ever. He broke in—barely—but the force-field is different on this side. He might not be able to solve all the equations. Manning knows we were looking for a force-field nullifier. So if Tezoc ordered us dead, Manning should have told him it was a bad idea, because we might be able to solve his problem. It just doesn't make sense that either Tezoc or Manning would order you to kill us."

"It doesn't have to," snapped Brice. "But for what it's worth, Manning seems to have a bug about you and your sister. For some reason he thinks you're more dangerous to us than all the Navy Seal and Army Ranger types on Colonel Sharp's team. He's studied your files extensively. He told us you've been thoroughly evaluated since joining the project. The evaluator found you both to be bright and creative, and also unusually prone to coming up with remarkable flashes of intuition and inspiration, especially under pressure. Manning is convinced that you two are capable of pulling all kinds of tricks from your sleeves." Brice scowled. "Personally, I think he's overestimated you by a lot. You came up with a good plan with the bugs," he admitted, "but everyone is lucky now and then. Anyway, Manning is certain that the force-field nullifier device that you describe doesn't exist. He ordered me to kill you and your sister, and told me if you brought something back and claimed it was a nullifier, it was a trick, and I should destroy it immediately."

"Manning is wrong!" insisted Ryan. "The technology *does* exist. And we found it. No tricks. Destroy it and you might be destroying your only chance of ever leaving this city. Don't you understand that?"

"Manning knows what he's doing," snapped Brice. "And I intend to carry out my orders. In fact, I've decided not to wait for your sister after all." He glanced suggestively at the assault rifle that was still pointed at Ryan "If you're inclined to say any prayers," he said icily, "you have exactly twenty seconds to say them."

And as Ryan stared into the soldier's cruel eyes, he knew Brice wouldn't hesitate to execute him and his sister, even though they were kids, and that no power on Earth could possibly get him to change his mind.

CHAPTER 19

Counterattack

"**R**egs!" broadcast Ryan, panicked. For the third time that day, it was time for plan B. If Regan hadn't stopped them from entering the building together, they'd both be dead by now.

"*Here,*" responded Regan immediately.

"*I'm in big trouble. We need to take this guy out right now or I'm dead. Get close to the entrance and have a flashbang ready.*"

"*Got it,*" broadcast Regan.

Ryan stumbled forward a few paces and crouched to the ground. "My head," he moaned, dropping to a sitting position. He put his hands tightly over his ears and rolled into a ball, still moaning. He covered his ears and eyes as tightly as possible with his arms and legs and rocked back and forth on the ground.

"Very, very tricky," said Brice, smirking. "I suppose now I'll just let my guard down, so you can—"

"*Regan, now!*" broadcast Ryan with all of his might, shutting his eyes as tightly as he could.

Regan stepped into the room behind them and tossed in a flashbang grenade, diving back out of the building before it hit the floor.

Brice turned just as it landed, but far too late to even brace himself for the blast. The flashbang explosion was intense beyond reason. While Ryan knew about these devices and what to expect, the reality was more jarring and terrifying than he could possibly have imagined. Even covered up as he was, Ryan thought the sound would shake him apart. The flash was as bright as a supernova, and although his face was pressed tightly against his legs the burst of light easily penetrating his closed eyelids. He was dazed and fought to recover from the shock of the blast.

He didn't have time to be dazed. He had to move now!

Ryan jumped to his feet.

Brice had caught the full brunt of the blast and was completely disoriented. The cruel mercenary was totally blind and deaf, giving Ryan the advantage, but he knew this wouldn't last for long. He crouched low behind Brice, who could neither hear nor see him as he readied his assault. With one lightning-quick motion, Ryan reached out, grabbed both of the merc's ankles, and yanked backwards with all of his might.

The mercenary was taken completely by surprise and crashed to the ground far too quickly to have time to get his arms out to cushion the fall. His face and forehead smashed into the floor, breaking his nose and knocking him unconscious. Regan arrived an instant later and covered Brice with the stun gun, but this was already unnecessary.

Ryan let out the breath he had been holding and tried to get his heart to stop racing. Regan said something to him but it was too soft to register through the ringing in his ears.

"Not hearing great yet," he explained telepathically. *"Use telepathy."*

"Hold his wrists," she broadcast.

Ryan nodded in understanding. Regan pulled a zip-strip from the merc's belt, and within seconds, like Davidenko before him, Brice's ankles and wrists were bound with sturdy plasticuffs.

Ryan found a combat knife strapped to Brice's leg, almost identical to the one he had taken from Davidenko. He removed it. Both he and Regan now had similar knives. They rushed to the large group of Prometheus scientists sprawled on the floor, whose hearing and vision had thankfully already returned to normal, and removed their gags. When this was completed, they quickly went to work sawing through Dr. Harris's sturdy plasticuff shackles.

Dr. Harris was white-haired and grandfatherly, with a

pear-shaped body, a beard, and inch-thick glasses. "Great work, kids," he said from his position on the floor.

Regan continued to work on his ankle cuffs while Ryan concentrated on freeing his hands. The mercs' knives were far better than the ones they had used earlier, and they were able to make short work of the tough plasticuffs that had bound Dr. Harris. They helped him to his feet and he stretched his legs gratefully.

"Thanks," he said in relief, as the siblings began working to free another scientist.

"You're very welcome," said Regan from the floor, continuing to work the knife. She glanced up at Dr. Harris and added sheepishly, "Sorry about the whole deaf and blindness thing."

Ryan nodded his agreement beside her.

"Well, at least now I know how bright the sun would appear—if I were *standing* on it," he quipped. He became serious once more. "Neither of you have anything to be sorry about. Your plan was effective—very effective—and none of us will suffer any permanent ill effects. We couldn't be more grateful."

Ryan shook his head. "Unfortunately, we're not out of this yet—by a long shot." He paused. "Where are Carl and his men?"

"About an hour ago Manning ordered two of his men to drive all the security people, except Carl, to where your father is. He said Tezoc wanted them to have a front-row seat to see his triumph." Dr. Harris lowered his eyes. "That's also when they took your mother."

Ryan nodded grimly. "You said all of security," he noted, "*except* Carl. Why didn't they take Carl?"

"According to Major Manning," replied Dr. Harris, "Tezoc had special plans for Carl."

"So where is he now?" said Ryan.

"Less than a minute before you arrived, Manning dumped Carl in the back of a Hauler and drove off. Before he left, he told Brice that Tezoc had changed his mind, and decided he wanted Carl at your father's location after all. He left Brice behind to guard us."

Ryan thought about this. Manning must have been driving the truck they had seen when they had arrived. And Carl was with him. Only they weren't heading to join Tezoc and his father. They had been driving in the *opposite* direction, toward the cavern—or maybe to Carl's headquarters building, which was right near the main entrance as well.

The siblings had now freed two other prisoners in addition to Dr. Harris, but quickly agreed telepathically that they couldn't waste even a second more. They handed their knives to the newly freed scientists. "Use these to free the others," said Ryan. "We need to go. Find another building to hide in within sight of this one. Have someone watch for us. If we aren't back here within two hours, assume we were captured and try to come up with a plan to rescue our parents and the security people."

"Dr Harris?" said one of the two scientists helplessly, looking for guidance.

"Do whatever they say," instructed the white-haired scientist. Ryan and Regan had proven themselves repeatedly and appeared to know far more about what was going on than he did. If anyone had earned the right to be in charge at that instant, it was them.

They thanked Dr. Harris and rushed off.

"Wait. I'm coming with you," he called after them.

They all loaded into the large passenger compartment of a Hauler and moved out at full speed to Ben Resnick's location in the city. Ryan drove since Dr. Harris didn't know the way.

Regan examined her watch. "We have about twelve minutes," she said anxiously.

"Dad won't make an attempt before then," said Ryan. "If he did figure out how to create an opening, he'll want as much time as possible to recheck his calculations."

As they drove they hastily brought Dr. Harris up to speed on recent events. His mouth dropped open in astonishment as they told him about their discovery of the nullifier, but the proper gratitude and congratulations they had earned would have to wait. Amazing!

"We should have enough time to stop the Hauler out of sight of the mercenaries and sneak close to them on foot," said Ryan. "Let's wait and see if our father can break through the barrier. If he does—at least if you can believe Tezoc—our mom won't be in any danger. We can stay hidden and then join the others to work on a rescue plan. If he fails, we'll be close enough to show ourselves immediately, before anything happens to our mom, and create Tezoc's exit for him with the nullifier."

"I can't see how even your father could create an exit in this short amount of time," said Dr. Harris grimly.

"We agree," said Regan. "We'll probably have to tell Tezoc about the nullifier."

Ryan frowned bleakly. "But Brice claims Manning ordered him to kill us and destroy anything we found. If these orders really did come from Tezoc, this is a suicide mission. The nullifier won't buy us a thing. In fact, Regan's convinced me that Tezoc already knows how to exit this city any time he wants to."

"Then why this game with your father and the barrier?"

"We have no idea," said Regan. "It doesn't make sense. But we don't have a choice. If Dad fails, we have to try to save Mom. Hopefully we're wrong and Tezoc was telling the truth and really does need an exit."

Ryan concentrated for all he was worth. He had to solve the puzzle. They continued to totally miss the big picture. Why had Manning taken Carl in the wrong direction? Was Manning working alone? Was he working *against* Tezoc? He and Regan had focused on Tezoc before. Maybe focusing on Manning would help. Ryan strained to his limits, trying to recall every encounter they had had with the short major, every observation they had made.

Ryan fought to process the ever-growing number of unconnected puzzle pieces that were filling his mind. He had to find the connection between them all as they swirled around like a thick soup in his brain. If he could take everything he had learned about Tezoc and Manning and the force-field and the invasion, and hold it in his mind at the same time, maybe he could somehow find the key to solve the puzzle.

"What a nightmare," said Dr. Harris miserably. "How could this have happened? Instead of a visit from the president, we get a visit from an alien madman."

"Visit from the president?" they both said at once.

When they had asked Carl to do a security sweep the week before, he had mentioned the president would be visiting soon, but he hadn't mentioned the date and they had forgotten all about it. "Are you saying he was supposed to visit today?" said Regan.

Dr. Harris nodded. "Yes. He was *supposed* to be visiting in two or three hours. That obviously won't be happening now," he noted.

Ryan's mind raced and adrenaline surged through his body. This had to be an important clue. It couldn't be a coincidence. He added this information to the cauldron in his brain and redoubled his efforts to solve the puzzle.

They turned a corner and stopped as Tezoc, Ben Resnick, and five mercenaries came into view. Just to Tezoc's left, Amanda Resnick and seven members of Prometheus security were bound on the ground. Instead of the array of powerful generators their father had used to tear a hole in the barrier before, there were only two small pieces of equipment, each the size of a large toaster. These were connected to a computer that sat between them.

They approached silently on foot, careful to stay out of sight. This wasn't difficult because Tezoc and his men had surrounded their father and their attention was riveted on him. He was about to begin his attempt to break through the barrier. He nodded his readiness but then decided to check the settings on the equipment one last time.

Dr. Harris and the siblings peered from behind a building about fifty yards from the group of invaders and their fellow team members. Ryan's brain tingled and his head began to ache from the monumental effort he was making to determine what Tezoc was really up to before it was too late. He was lucky his earlier headache had gone away, although he realized he could have cured it instantly with the alien medical device as he had done for his sister.

Regan's headache!

As soon as he thought about her headache as well as his own, he knew this was an important clue. He quickly added it to the others.

They had both gotten headaches. What did this mean? *Think!* he ordered himself.

His mind raced furiously, churning through different possibilities.

Bingo! His eyes went wide.

In a flash of inspiration he connected all the dots. Finally.

But as he looked up, he realized in horror that his father was standing over the equipment again, his right hand reaching down to turn it all on and begin his attempt to create a hole in the city's shield.

"No!" screamed Ryan at the top of his lungs.

He sprinted out from his hiding place and waved his arms in front of him. "Dad, stop!" he screamed as he ran. "Turn that on and you'll kill us all."

CHAPTER 20

A Startling Assertion

B en Resnick had been an instant away from turning on the equipment when he heard his son's voice in the distance. He was just able to jerk his hand away in time.

The mercenaries responded rapidly. Fanning out at a run, they seized Ryan and discovered Dr. Harris and Regan moments later, bringing all three to face Tezoc.

The imposingly tall, lanky alien was seething. He pointed at Ryan. "Captain Hanly," he barked to the muscular soldier beside him. "Kill him."

The captain frowned. "He's just a kid."

"I said kill him," barked Tezoc. "I have my reasons. Don't you ever question my orders!"

The captain pointed his rifle at Ryan but it was clear he was still uncertain. Even so, Ryan knew he had only seconds to make his point. "Don't do it," he pleaded.

"Think! Why did I come out of hiding just now? To warn you, that's why." He pointed to the towering alien. "Tezoc plans to kill you all. Let me save your lives."

Ryan blurted this all out in a single breath and as a single sentence, knowing that Hanly could decide to pull the trigger at any time.

Hanly's weapon wavered.

"I will not say this again, Captain," said Tezoc icily. "Kill him now."

"Things aren't what they seem," said Ryan hurriedly. "Ask yourself, why does he want me dead? I'm unarmed. He's afraid of what I have to say, that's why. You're placing blind trust in a madman who isn't even human! Give me five minutes to save your lives."

Ryan's rapid-fire words were spoken almost at the same pace as those of an auctioneer. The situation was tense, and he needed to get his arguments out before anyone decided to follow Tezoc's orders. "I'm your prisoner. You can shoot me whenever you want. What's the hurry?"

As Ryan spoke the mercenaries moved closer to him and Tezoc. Several of them had become intrigued by what he was saying. Why *did* Tezoc want the boy dead so badly?

"If this boy still has a pulse in three seconds," thundered Tezoc, "every last one of you can kiss your three million dollars goodbye."

"You can't spend money when you're dead, which

is what will happen if you listen to Tezoc," blurted out Ryan breathlessly. "If I'm wrong, you can shoot me five minutes from now. But if I'm right, killing me now is as good as killing yourselves. I don't have a weapon. All I have are words. Think! Why does he want to shut me up so badly?"

While Ryan was speaking, Tezoc shuffled a step or two closer to Ben Resnick and the equipment. Noticing this, two mercenaries on that side moved closer together, pointedly blocking his access.

The tide was beginning to turn! Ryan knew he was reaching the five mercenaries. Several of them raised eyebrows and glanced at each other meaningfully. The boy posed no danger. Why was Tezoc so afraid of what he might say?

Hanly considered Ryan's argument and knew his fellow mercenaries were doing the same. Even though Tezoc was acting irrationally, Hanly was very loyal to the alien and found it a struggle to even consider disobeying his orders. But if the boy was right, his life depended on doing so now. Besides, he told himself, he wasn't really refusing an order as much as he was delaying it for five minutes. Finally having come to a firm decision, Hanly turned his weapon away from the boy and trained it on Tezoc. "I say let's hear the kid out."

There were nods and low murmurs of agreement all around. Hanley now had the full support of the soldiers—at least temporarily.

"You have five minutes," said Hanly evenly. "Use them wisely."

"The kid's got nothing!" bellowed Tezoc. "Whatever he says is a lie! If trying to create an exit out of this city will kill us all, why am I still standing here? He has a great imagination and he's quite clever, but he's trying to sell you a bill of goods. Just remember you're listening to nothing but a fantasy story."

"Well I, for one, am curious to hear this fantasy story of his," said Hanly. "None of us are stupid, regardless of what you might think. You can't get this far in the soldiering business without being able to think for yourself. *We'll* decide if what the boy has to say makes sense. So no more interruptions!" he said with finality.

Hanly knew he had to be forceful with Tezoc, even though he didn't want to be, because all of his experience told him it was vital that he listen to Ryan. But he had every intention of making it up to the alien later—more than making it up to him. Despite this small hiccup, he was not about to let Tezoc down.

Tezoc fumed but said nothing further.

Hanly nodded at Ryan. "Go ahead," he said, and then, frowning deeply, added, "Oh, and son, Tezoc makes a good point about his still being here when we're all about to commit—as you describe it—mass suicide. I'll be quite interested to hear your explanation for this."

"The explanation is very simple," replied Ryan. He pointed to the tall alien. "You see, that man isn't Tezoc Zoron," he said with absolute conviction. "The real Tezoc Zoron has no intention of being here when we destroy ourselves."

CHAPTER 21

A Convincing Argument

Ryan's bold assertion hit the gathering like a bombshell, stunning mercenaries and members of the Prometheus team alike.

"Tezoc was right," snapped Hanly angrily once the commotion this caused had died down. "This *is* a fantasy story."

Ryan quickly raised his right hand, palm outward. "Let me finish," he said. "I know it sounds crazy. You said I had five minutes."

Hanly thought for a few seconds and then nodded. "This had better be good."

Ryan had been holding his breath and exhaled loudly in relief. Beside him, Regan was thinking furiously, assuming he was right and using this as the key to connect the dots for herself.

"Okay," began Ryan. "What do we all know about Tezoc?"

"I thought you said this guy *isn't* Tezoc," interjected one of the mercs.

"Don't worry about that for a second," said Ryan in frustration. He paused and began again. "What do we know about Tezoc? We know he's an advanced alien. And we can guess he has amazing intelligence and abilities, even among his own kind, because he was able to escape an escape-proof prison and come to this city. And he plans very carefully and doesn't leave anything to chance."

Ryan paused to let the group digest what he had said. "Finally," he added, "we know he has telepathic abilities."

Ryan could tell from the group's body language they agreed with everything he had said so far. He knew that his very life depended on his ability to make a convincing argument.

"Tezoc let everyone know that he can use these abilities to sense and detect the minds of adults around him," he continued. "But what if he can do a lot more with these powers than he's letting on? What if he can use them to enter people's thoughts? What if, for one person at a time, he's able to control them completely? Turn them into his puppets—extensions of himself?"

"And your evidence?" said Hanly, still attentively holding his weapon on Tezoc.

"My evidence is that this is the only way that any of this makes sense—so it has to be right. Let me review everything that's happened here from the beginning and you'll understand what I mean. Eight days ago Tezoc escaped and arrived in this city."

"How do you know this happened exactly eight days ago?" asked a mercenary.

"I guess I can't tell them about the telepathic warning," Ryan broadcast to his sister, *"or they'll think I'm crazy for sure."* Aloud he said, "Because my sister and I saw something funny last Friday that we thought might be an alien. Maybe he was here before last Friday, but I know he was here then."

"Go on," said Hanly.

"Because we thought we saw an alien we asked Carl . . . Colonel Sharp," he corrected, "to conduct a security sweep of the city. He didn't find anything. But later we learned that he had lost his memory of that day. He didn't remember our conversation and he didn't remember ordering a sweep."

Ryan raised his eyebrows. "And while we're talking about the colonel's memory loss, have any of you forgotten stuff that happened to you during the past week? Found out you did things you don't remember doing?"

From the funny looks on the invaders' faces, Ryan knew he had scored points—vital points. His gamble had paid off in a big way. If he was wrong about this, they would have been more resistant to further arguments. But he was right!

All five of the mercs nodded with troubled looks in their eyes. Each had had brief memory losses they had explained away to themselves. But none of them had discussed this, even with each other. So how had the boy known? They looked at Ryan with a new respect, now very inclined to take him seriously. Whatever story he was telling, it wasn't *all* imagination. And the implications of these periodic memory losses were quite disturbing.

Ryan nodded back at the mercs. "A pretty bizarre coincidence, don't you think," he said. "But I'll come back to this in a second. Let me continue with what I think happened in the order it happened. I think the colonel *did* find Tezoc during that sweep. Or Tezoc found him. As I said, I think Tezoc can totally control another person—completely take over their body and mind. But not easily. My guess is he can only control one person at a time—and that this takes major concentration and effort on his part."

"These are fascinating guesses," admitted Hanly. "But I still don't see how you came to your conclusions."

"First, Colonel Sharp lost his memory of the entire first day that Tezoc was here. Second, Tezoc had to leave this city to recruit his team and then break back in with all of you. This should have been impossible to do without tripping any alarms, even with advanced alien technology. The only way he could have done it is if the head of security were helping him. The only way." Ryan paused. "But Colonel Sharp would *never* help him," he said with absolute conviction. "No way. Not even if his life depended on it."

"I know of the colonel's reputation," volunteered one of the mercs. "He is said to be a man of impeccable honor." The soldier grinned and then added, "I guess nobody's perfect."

Hanly nodded. "I'm also familiar with his reputation. And I agree that Colonel Sharp would never have sold out this project." He paused, a concerned look now on his face. "When Tezoc laid out his plan for us, he had all the security codes, knew all the fail-safes, knew when guard shifts changed and even the personal habits of the guards. He mapped out a flawless strategy. We joked that he knew as much about security as the man who ran it, but we let ourselves believe he had acquired it using advanced technology."

Ryan shook his head. "The colonel helped him without knowing it. Tezoc invaded his mind and controlled him like a puppet. Then Tezoc erased his memory. It's the only possible explanation."

Ryan waited for this to sink in and then continued. "Once Tezoc left the city, he took control of a super-tall man who he used from a distance to do everything else. The first thing he had his tall puppet do was to recruit his army. And you're all here, so it's obvious he succeeded. But think about it. He shouldn't have. If you were all thinking normally, would you ever have trusted him? Yes, Tezoc probably had a ton of money. Being able to completely control someone—say a bank president—can help you become rich very fast," noted Ryan. "But he made all kinds of crazy claims. He said— or had his puppet say at any rate—that he was an alien. He told you there was an alien city deep underground. And he claimed to have security information that should have been impossible to get." Ryan paused. "But you couldn't have known if there really was an alien city until you actually stepped through the entrance in the cavern. And your lives would depend on his information about security being totally accurate and up to date. If you were acting normally, you'd think he was insane, or at least you'd be extremely suspicious. Would you really risk your life to attack an alien city—taking his word that there was such a thing in the first place—without carefully checking out who he really was and where he got his information?"

Heads were shaking in disbelief all around. The boy made some excellent points and they were beginning to seriously question their own behavior.

"If Tezoc was wrong about anything," continued Ryan, "you'd fail instantly. And even if there really was an alien city, and you were able to capture it, you had to know you'd have to fight off the country's entire army to keep it."

The mercenaries were blinking now as if coming out of a fog. They were in complete confusion. Why *had* they signed on for this? Why *had* they followed Tezoc so blindly? When they broke into the city, they had truly kicked a hornet's nest. The kid was right. How could they have failed to realize that even success would only buy them a war they couldn't possibly win?

Hanly voiced what everyone was thinking. "You're absolutely right. No amount of money in the world could have gotten us to agree to this. Under normal circumstances," he added pointedly.

Ryan nodded. "Exactly. You never would have agreed to it—unless you had a strong push. Unless Tezoc snuck into your minds and searched your memories. Then he would know exactly what arguments would work on you. He probably controlled you during this time and then erased your memory of it. Even that wouldn't be enough. He would have had to slightly adjust your mind, your way of thinking. Make you more open to his arguments. Change you so you'd be greedier than normal; less suspicious than normal. Change you so you wouldn't think as clearly as normal. Even increase your feelings of loyalty to him once you agreed to join him."

The soldiers looked ill. They knew Ryan was right. It was the only way to explain how they had totally lost the judgment that had kept them alive for so many years in a dangerous profession. It was the only way to explain why they were so fiercely loyal to the alien. Why questioning any of Tezoc's orders, no matter how strange or irrational they were, had been so incredibly difficult for them to do.

Ryan continued to press home the point relentlessly. "Captain Hanly. You were about to shoot an unarmed kid. You didn't, but you were pretty close. I know you're a mercenary, but I can't believe this is part of the mercenary code."

Hanly shook his head in horror. He knew Ryan was right. He had resisted Tezoc's order, but under normal circumstances he would have flat out refused it. He wasn't a saint but he didn't shoot unarmed children. Perhaps psychos like Brice might, but not him. But he had been close. He had almost pulled the trigger.

"Tezoc made you more loyal to him and more likely to follow his orders," explained Ryan. "Fortunately for me—for all of us—you were still yourself enough that you didn't do it. I think he has to be very close to someone—or even in contact with them—when he takes control of them. After that they can be separated and he can still keep control. But he can't seize control from a distance." Ryan paused. "He couldn't give up control of his tall puppet here to take control of someone else just now. Not from a distance."

"How do you know that?" asked Hanly.

Ryan shrugged. "If he could have, he would have done it already," he replied simply.

Ryan knew he had completely won the mercs over. He was no longer the enemy. They were hanging on his every word and knew he was right. They were horrified to realize that Tezoc had entered their minds and manipulated them against their will.

Hanly signaled to two mercenaries closest to Tezoc. "Let's make sure he can't go anywhere," he said.

The soldiers immediately went to work binding Tezoc. He didn't complain and he didn't resist. His eyes were open but he was very still, as if he were moments away from falling asleep.

"While you're at it," said Regan. "Do you think you could free the prisoners?"

Hanly considered. "I don't see why not. I guess in a way we're all on the same team now."

Ryan frowned deeply. While it was great that the mercenaries were now on their team, at least for the time being, he knew something that Hanly did not. He knew that their team was losing. Losing badly.

In fact, he was almost certain that their team had already lost.

CHAPTER 22

Connecting the Dots

After the prisoners' plasticuffs were cut, the entire group relocated so everyone was more comfortable. The five mercenaries sat around the smooth, yellow table. After having been prisoners for so long, the newly freed members of the Prometheus team preferred to stand, relieved to finally be able to do so.

Dan Walpus was doing well under the circumstances. The mercenaries had allowed Miguel to dress his wound properly and the bleeding had been staunched completely. Regan pulled out her alien medical device and pointed it at Dan's arm, activating the accelerated wound healing and pain relief functions. If they could find a way to get out of this mess, Dan would be fine.

Amanda and Ben Resnick had joined their children and Dr. Harris in the middle of the crowd, at the very center of attention. The teary hugs the kids had received from their mother and father had taken almost as long as the removal of the prisoner's plasticuff restraints. But after only a few minutes, everyone was ready to resume.

Ryan stood. "So Tezoc enters the city and takes control of Colonel Sharp," he continued. "He definitely has control of him when he leaves Prometheus and probably also on the way back in. He takes from Carl's mind and computer everything he needs to know about the security setup and how to beat it. He gets back in the city with his army. Then what happens?" Ryan addressed the question to Captain Hanly.

The captain was still the mercenary nearest to him, although he was now seated at the table with his weapon out of sight. "Then Tezoc knocks everyone in the city unconscious," he answered. "And we are easily able to collect them without a fight."

"How did he do it?" asked Ryan.

Hanly shrugged. "He told us he used alien technology. We believed him."

"Again, he had adjusted your minds to believe almost anything he told you. I'll bet he used another aspect of his mental abilities to do the job. Maybe he can send a telepathic wave that knocks out everyone in its path. Maybe he can affect the sleep centers of the brain."

"You're probably right," said Hanly. "I never did see him use any kind of device."

Hanly's lips pursed together in thought. "I understand why he took control of Colonel Sharp—it was the only way to break out of the city, and then back into it, undetected. But why go to the trouble of controlling someone and pretending to be them the entire time he was on Earth?"

"Tezoc is very smart and very careful," replied Ryan. "He found a really tall mercenary to be his puppet before he recruited the rest of you. A man so giant people would be more likely to believe he was an alien. That way, the real Tezoc could control everything without anyone knowing his true identity. And if he made any mistakes, this tall human would be everyone's main target, not him. If Carl and his security people had managed to escape and stop his puppet, thinking they had stopped him, he would still be a step ahead of everyone."

"So who is Tezoc really?" asked Dr. Harris.

"My sister and I captured Davidenko and Brice. But what other mercenary isn't here right now?"

Since there were only five mercenaries present, everyone had already noted the absence of Tezoc's second in command, Major Manning. Several in the group muttered his name at the same time.

Ryan nodded. "That's right. Manning said he was coming here long ago, but he hasn't. He's the true alien. Manning set up a Tezoc character to be in charge and he took the job of second in command. When his tall Tezoc puppet first spoke with the prisoners, Manning never said a word, and was so still most of the time he almost could have been asleep. It must be hard work to see through the eyes of another person: to use their brain, their mouth, and concentrate on your own activities at the same time. The alien can do it, but it's probably much easier for him when he and the human he's controlling aren't active at the same time."

Ryan turned again to face Captain Hanly. "Tell me," he said on a hunch. "What did the man you thought was Tezoc do here for the past six hours?"

"He had bursts of activity during which he would direct the men and give orders, but the majority of the time he just sat perfectly still, staring off into space."

"And you didn't find that strange?" asked Ryan.

"No," replied one of the mercs, frowning. "Obviously more proof that we were conditioned not to ask too many questions."

"Again, he probably didn't want to handle himself and another person at the same time very often," said Ryan. "When his Tezoc character was active, Manning would want to be as inactive as possible. The opposite would also be true. When Manning needed to focus all of his concentration on being himself, he would have his Tezoc puppet here stare off into space."

Ben Resnick nodded beside his son. "This would explain why Tezoc and Manning immediately separated into two camps, with Tezoc in charge of one and Manning the other. If they were together, there was more of a chance someone would notice this pattern of behavior."

"Exactly," said Ryan.

"Is this what led you to your conclusion, Ryan?" asked his mother.

"This was only one of many clues. I'm sure you remember when Manning turned and fired on Captain Walpus." As he had done with Carl, Ryan felt it was important to use Dan's military rank rather than his first name in the presence of other soldiers, even mercenaries. "The Tezoc character claimed he had given Manning a signal," said Ryan. "But I was watching. He didn't give any signal."

One of the mercenaries nodded. "I was watching also, and there was no signal. But I didn't question it. I should have. Tezoc did a nice job of turning us into obedient fools."

Several of the mercenaries nodded in agreement, scowling bitterly.

"The shooting was another clue," continued Ryan. "Manning was concentrating on controlling his Tezoc puppet when Captain Walpus regained consciousness. But even while distracted, Manning's mental radar finally did pick up the captain. That's how he knew exactly where to shoot, even though his back was completely turned at the time. Manning must have been the alien—the one with mental abilities."

The mercenaries discussed Manning and Tezoc for almost a minute, bringing up other examples of strange behaviors they had witnessed.

THE PROMETHEUS PROJECT: CAPTURED

"*So what finally helped you put the pieces all to-gether?*" broadcast Regan while the mercs were talking.

"*When we were in the mercs' headquarters, preparing to throw the globes, we felt telepathic energy,*" explained Ryan, "*even though Tezoc wasn't there. But we never really thought any more about it. Then I remembered you telling me you had gotten a headache there. I never mentioned it, but so had I. What are the chances of both of us getting an instant headache at the exact same time? The last time this happened was when the Teacher was communicating telepathically with us but using an incompatible frequency. This time it happened when we were both standing next to Manning. Again, since Tezoc wasn't even there, Manning must have been the source of the telepathy.*"

"*Great thinking, Ryan,*" broadcast his sister admiringly.

"*Thanks,*" he replied. "*But I couldn't have solved it without you. In fact, I wouldn't have even known there was a puzzle to be solved. You were the one who alerted me that we were missing the big picture.*"

The mercs conversation had died out so Ryan continued aloud. "The final clue," he said, unable to bring up the clues he had just shared with his sister, "was how strangely the nanobots acted. They had never retreated while they were in the middle of a repair before. Never. But they did so, coincidentally, just seconds before my plan was about to work. Several of them even stopped dead in the middle of the floor, which has never happened either. They must have been given a telepathic command to retreat. Manning was the only one who could have done it. Again, Tezoc wasn't even in the building at the time, and Manning was the only mercenary not panicking at the sight of the nanobots."

Dr. Harris nodded. "Your analysis is excellent, Ryan. I'm sure you're right about Major Manning."

"So where is he now?" asked Ben Resnick. "And what is he doing?"

"I'm not exactly sure where he is," said Ryan. "But I think he's probably in or near the cavern."

Ryan paused. "But I am sure about what he's doing," he said grimly. "He's about to take a gigantic step closer to ruling the entire planet."

CHAPTER 23

A Nightmarish Future

"Bravo, kids," said the Tezoc imposter from out of nowhere. He had been as still as a reptile for some time. He smiled and added, "I was right not to underestimate you."

A chill came over the entire gathering along with an eerie silence. Not even the sound of breathing could be heard. Everyone immediately turned to face the man they had thought was Tezoc.

"Is this Major Manning talking?" asked Dr. Harris.

The man laughed. "Who else? The man in front of you was—and will be again after I'm done with him—Lieutenant Mike Adams. As Ryan guessed, I am in full control of him. You know me as Major Manning, but my real name is, indeed, Tezoc Zoron. Since I'm not human, I couldn't resist choosing a name with the word "man" in it as an alias. Man-ning. Get it?" He laughed, very pleased with himself. "Since I am now in complete control of this mercenary's brain and body, for the time being, refer to him as Tezoc."

"Why don't you tell us what's going on," invited Dr. Harris.

"No, no. I wouldn't think of it. The boy is doing a fine job. Why don't we let him continue. At this point, there's no reason you shouldn't know the true extent of my genius."

"Is everything I've said so far right?" asked Ryan.

"Almost," replied Tezoc. "Almost. Your conclusions about my ability to control people, and alter their emotions and centers of reason to suit my needs, are quite accurate. But you aren't giving me my full due. In addition to my other talents, I'm among the greatest inventors of my kind. My species has some slight mental abilities, but nothing like I've demonstrated here. During my years of preparation, I invented a device that dramatically amplifies my mental abilities, more than a hundredfold. The device is tuned precisely to humans. In fact, I chose your species because you are especially susceptible to my mental energy."

For just an instant a confused look crossed the tall mercenary's face. "It still baffles me why I can't affect you or your sister, though." He paused for a few seconds in thought, frowning, but finally decided to continue.

"My invention can also direct mental energy to the sleep centers of human brains," he boasted. "Once I saw that Dr. Harris was with you, it was obvious you managed to free the Prometheus scientists I left with Captain Brice in the other building. While I suspect that all seventeen of them together couldn't cause me as much trouble as you and your annoying sister, it wouldn't do to have them running around the city unguarded. So I took the trouble to locate all of their minds a few minutes ago," he continued. "You should know that they are all now sleeping like babies a few miles north of you."

Dr. Harris frowned. He had wondered how the other scientists the kids had freed were faring. Not all that well, it seemed. On the other hand, there were fates far worse than mere sleep.

"But I digress, Ryan," said Tezoc. "Why don't you continue with your analysis."

All eyes turned toward Ryan. He took a moment to gather his thoughts and then said, "It was Regan who first realized something was very, very wrong. She figured the race that built this city as an outpost would've made it easy for authorized visitors to leave. And we knew that Tezoc was very smart and very careful. He had even beaten Qwervy portal security somehow. Regan couldn't believe that he could do all these things that seemed impossible and then do something stupid like trap himself inside the city."

"The girl is an excellent judge of talent," boasted Tezoc. "I'll give her that."

Ryan ignored him. "Regan was sure he was lying. She was sure he could exit the force-field anytime, and anywhere, he wanted. So by sealing the city everyone else was trapped, but *he* could leave whenever he wanted. He told us that he closed our entrance because he was worried outside security would send the army after him. But by controlling Colonel Sharp, he could have reassured outside security that all was well down here. He could have bought himself plenty of time."

Ryan stared at Tezoc. "Well?" he said.

Tezoc smiled. "Very good," he said. "You have a knack for this. This is exactly what I did. Using your Colonel Sharp, I dismissed the outside security people, telling them that the city and cavern were being locked down for twenty-four hours while tests were being conducted on the electronic security systems."

"You told the Prometheus prisoners that you were worried about the military coming after you," continued Ryan. "And that you *weren't* worried about the Qwervy at all. The truth is just the opposite, isn't it?" he insisted. "You aren't the least bit worried about the human military. You're worried about the Qwervy being able to come after you through the portals."

"Yes, yes, yes," spat Tezoc. "The almighty Qwervy. While I don't expect them to discover that Earth is off their grid for some time, it pays to be cautious. There is always a slight chance that I'm wrong about that. And while I despise them, I have to admit they're the only ones who can stop me. At least for the moment," he added defiantly.

"You said you wanted this city as a base of operations," pressed Ryan. "But this isn't true either. You can take over Earth without it. You want it destroyed so the Qwervy can't come through after you. And you planned to trick us into destroying the city, and *ourselves* with it."

"A brilliant plan, don't you think," boasted Tezoc. "The city can only be destroyed from the inside, and I didn't want to leave behind anyone who knew anything about me. Fooling you into destroying yourselves was just too perfect to pass up, allowing me to kill two birds with one stone. Since I wouldn't need Lieutenant Adams to play the role of alien anymore, he was also expendable."

Tezoc paused. "The equipment I gave your father is not set to the frequencies he thinks. If he had tried to create an opening in the shield he would have caused a chain reaction. As you predicted, it would have destroyed the city. About three hours after he turned the equipment on the entire city would have collapsed in on itself and disappeared."

"And you would have been long gone by then," said Ryan in disgust.

"Exactly. End of city. End of mercenaries. End of Prometheus team. And no portals for the Qwervy to travel through to interfere."

Tezoc's plan may have been utterly ruthless, but there was no denying that it would also have been extremely effective.

"Once you had my sister and me," said Ryan, "why did you let us go? You didn't need a nullifier."

"Very true, but no one else knew that. If I didn't let you go on your wild goose chase, the prisoners might have become suspicious of my true intentions. Besides, while you're both very clever, I knew you couldn't threaten me alone. This way I kept you separated from the others—so you couldn't mastermind any clever escapes and they wouldn't feel the need to be heroic to protect you. Adults in your culture have a very overdeveloped sense of protectiveness toward children. By pretending to treat you fairly, I knew they would continue to cooperate." Tezoc paused. "I also didn't think it was possible for you to escape from Davidenko," he added irritably. "Apparently, I was wrong about that."

"There was something else you were wrong about," said Regan. "Destroying this city wouldn't have kept you safe from the Qwervy. Once they realized what happened, they would just send a ship here and plant another nanobot. The nanobot would quickly multiply and rebuild the city—*and* the portals—in no time."

"Are you positive about that?" said Tezoc smugly. "I'm sure you remember that when several of the nanobots stopped dead—on my telepathic command, I might add, as your brother guessed—I collected them. Doing so was always part of my plan, you just provided me with an earlier opportunity. Now why do you suppose I would want to do that?"

"To study them?" guessed Regan.

"To reprogram them," said Tezoc with a malevolent grin. "A little something I learned how to do in prison back home. You see, the Qwervy are far too overconfident. They don't classify information about their outpost cities—including information on programming the nanobots—because in their unrivaled arrogance, they are certain no unauthorized person could ever travel to an outpost city to use it. Well I have!" barked Tezoc. "Right under their noses. And now I can program the nanobots to build anything I want—or to destroy what I want. I can make sure the Qwervy never rebuild their outpost, never have access to this planet again."

"But we didn't destroy the city," pointed out Dr. Harris. "Or ourselves. These kids saved us from that. So your plan is ruined."

Tezoc laughed and shook his head. When his laughter finally stopped, the lines of his face hardened to a fierce scowl. "Saved you? *You aren't going anywhere!*" he thundered. "Ruined! You think they *ruined* my plan? They have barely disrupted it. These kids just bought you a week or so before I can come back and finish the job. And there won't be a single thing any of you can do to stop me!"

"We won't have to," said Dr. Harris defiantly. "You

may have bought yourself some time with our outside security, but the military *will* learn of this very shortly and come after you, no matter where you go."

This time Tezoc laughed even harder. He looked at Ryan, still laughing, and said, "Tell him. Tell him what's going to happen next. Go ahead," he demanded.

All eyes turned toward Ryan who was rapidly becoming sick to his stomach. He wished he could avoid telling the entire group just how dire, and hopeless, their situation was. But he had no choice. "Tezoc chose the timing for his invasion very carefully," he said miserably. "When he first took control of Colonel Sharp, he learned something from his mind. Something that made this day critically important to him."

Ryan waited, knowing it would only be a matter of seconds before someone made the right connection.

"The president!" whispered Cam Kincaid in horror, suddenly looking as ill as Ryan. Several others gasped as the horrifying implications hit them like a fist to the gut.

Ryan nodded. "The president is supposed to be flown here in *Marine One* for a visit in a few hours. But the Secret Service won't let him even take off until they're positive everything here is secure. Before they give him the okay, they first have to meet with the head of Prometheus security to get a face-to-face report."

Tezoc's lips curled up into a self-satisfied smile. "And they will have their face-to-face meeting with Colonel

Sharp," he said smugly. "In fact, the colonel is here with me now, temporarily unconscious, right in front of where your entrance used to be. In just a few minutes, I will relinquish control of Lieutenant Adams here and retake control of the colonel. He will reassure the Secret Service that all is well." He smiled malevolently. "After all, I want the president to feel completely safe landing here for his tour."

Amanda Resnick's eyes widened in understanding. "That's why you threatened any merc who as much as scratched Carl," she said. "You needed him to lure the president here. If he was shot or injured, the Secret Service would be suspicious."

"It's nice to see that someone is finally catching up to the kids," said Tezoc dryly. "I have to say, it's about time." He paused. "The boy was correct. When I first enter and control a person's mind, I need to be very close to them. That's why I'm so looking forward to Colonel Sharp introducing me to the president." He laughed once again. "Do you still think the military will be coming after me, Dr. Harris?"

Dr. Harris was aghast. He couldn't see any flaws in the alien's plan. He would soon control the President of the United States, and there seemed nothing anyone could do about it.

"And let's face it," continued Tezoc. "When I have total control of the president's mind and body, *I am the president!* The power I'll be able to wield will be staggering. And it won't just be the president. Through him, I'll have access to any world leader I want. To control. To alter. And it keeps getting better. You see, when I built my invention, I didn't have access to any humans to experiment on. Now that I do, I should be able to increase its effectiveness considerably. I will still only be able to control one person at a time, but I'll be able to do what I did with the mercenaries far more effectively. I'll be able to alter the minds of massive groups of people at once, instilling blind devotion to me, unquestioning loyalty. Within a year I'll be the absolute ruler of the entire planet."

Even the mercenaries were horrified at the nightmarish picture of the future painted by the crazed but brilliant alien. And there was absolutely no doubt he could do it.

"But why?" asked Dr. Harris, frowning deeply. "Why do this?"

"Spoken like a true sheep," said Tezoc with contempt. "Just as a sheep will never understand the wolf's need to hunt, you will never understand the pleasure I will get from bending an entire species to my will. From having absolute power. From being able to crush anyone on this planet beneath my heal on a whim. This is something I could never have achieved on Morca. On Earth, I will rule with an iron fist; the bravest of men will cringe at the mention of my name," he thundered menacingly. "And it's even more satisfying knowing the

185

detestable Qwervy made it all possible. If I had escaped prison and stayed on Morca, I would have been recaptured fairly quickly by my own people, even without the help of their new alien friends. But the existence of the Qwervy's portals changed everything. By using them, I could escape Morca altogether. I could avoid recapture. And I could claim a planet for my own."

Dr. Harris looked nauseous. "Why us? Why Earth?"

"Oh, don't take it personally. You just happened to fit the bill. I needed a planet that was advanced but not yet a member of the galactic community. One whose people had a fairly close resemblance to Morcans. And one whose people would be particularly susceptible to my telepathic abilities once they were sufficiently amplified. Out of the thousands and thousands of civilizations and planets I considered, only yours was perfect for my needs. Congratulations."

"But what will you—"

"Enough!" snapped Tezoc. "As much as I would love to stay and chat, I'm about to be very busy. I have a certain colonel to take control of once again, and important people to see. Regan was right, of course. I know the telepathic codes to open the barrier anywhere I want. And now it's time to use them to step through to the cavern and turn the generators back on so Colonel Sharp and I can use the elevator. The colonel had them shut off during the security lock-down and they'll take ten or fifteen minutes to boot up." He smiled. "I'm sure no one would want Colonel Sharp to be late for his meeting with the Secret Service. That would be rude." With a final, cruel smile, he added, "Wait here. I'll be back before you know it to destroy you and the city."

With that, the siblings felt a wave of highly amplified telepathic force, and their parents, Dr. Harris, seven members of Prometheus security, six mercenaries, and the tall man who had been Tezoc's puppet all crumpled to the floor around them like rag dolls, unconscious.

CHAPTER 24

A Critical Mission

Ryan and Regan gasped as the entire group collapsed around them. Once again, the alteration the Teacher had made in their mental frequencies that allowed them to be telepathic with each other also made them immune to Tezoc's mental energy.

As startling and unnerving as it was to suddenly find themselves the only two members of the team still standing, they were energized by Tezoc's last words.

They still had a chance!

Tezoc had revealed he needed ten minutes or so to revive the generators and get the elevator operational again.

They were not beaten yet. They could still stop him!

But every second counted.

They shook their father hard, hoping to rouse him from his deep slumber, but they could not awaken him. All the others in the group were sound asleep as well.

Regan rifled through Hanly's belt, removing a flash-bang grenade to replace the one she had used. She removed another small stun gun, exactly matching the one she carried in her pocket, and handed it to Ryan, along with several zip-strips.

In seconds they were speeding to the cavern in a Hauler as fast as it would go.

"We have two advantages over Major Manning," began Ryan. "First—"

"I think we need to be careful not to still think of him as Manning," interrupted Regan.

Ryan looked at her quizzically.

"We need to always have it in our heads that he's Tezoc, an alien, and the mastermind behind all of this," she pointed out. "Since he is alien, we can't be sure how strong and fast he might be. If we keep thinking of him as a regular human named Manning, we might not be as worried about him as we need to be."

"Regular human?" said Ryan, rolling his eyes. "I don't know about you, but even when I thought that guy was human he scared me to death. I'm not sure it's possible for me to be more worried about him," he said. "But I do get your point. I won't call him Manning anymore." He paused. "As I was saying, we have two advantages. First, he thinks he's totally safe. He has no idea we can come through the barrier after him. There's no way he could have guessed we found a force-field nullifier in the last few hours."

"He'll be surprised all right."

"Our telepathy is our other advantage. We can use it to work together without him knowing it."

The siblings immediately began discussing possible strategies, keeping their advantages in mind. It took them only a few minutes to agree on a plan they thought might work. They certainly wouldn't have to wait long to find out for sure.

Eight minutes after they had left the unconscious adults they arrived at where they knew the cavern was located. Although it couldn't be seen through the force-field barrier, the cavern, and the real Tezoc, were waiting for them on the other side.

Over the past several months they had come to know the cavern extremely well. It was the size of a baseball stadium. One half was nearly empty while the other half was packed with heavy machinery and scientific equipment of every kind. Rows of huge excavation vehicles that had been used to dig out the cavern were parked next to backup lasers and microwave generators. A large electrical generator provided power for everything in the cavern, including the elevator and all security measures. A backup generator was also located in the crowded half of the cavern, always standing at the ready in case of emergencies. Heavy, multicolored cables snaked across the floor bringing power to the cavern's lighting and other systems, although the lighting system also had internal battery backups in case both generators were out for any reason, as they were now.

Regan patted the light-red crystal nullifier in her pocket and took a deep breath. It was all up to them now. No mission in history had ever been more important. They had to find a way to stop Tezoc.

The price of failure was unthinkable.

They moved to a section of the barrier they hoped would open into the cluttered part of the cavern. They prepared to step through the force-field, bracing themselves to react instantly to any surprises they might encounter as they did so. As planned, Regan held a flashbang grenade while Ryan gripped a stun gun in his right hand.

They stepped through on Regan's signal.

The nullifier worked perfectly. They found themselves behind a large excavator as they had hoped, perfectly concealed from the rest of the cavern. So far, so good.

They peered from behind the vehicle carefully. Tezoc and Carl were still there! They were both standing calmly near the elevator. Other than this, the cavern was deserted.

Carl's plasticuff restraints had been removed and his weapons and security gear had been fully returned to him. A sleek, high-tech walkie-talkie now hung from his belt along with his pistol, knife, and other weapons.

This could only mean that Tezoc was now in full control of him as they had expected.

With a loud buzz the indicator light on top of the main power generator changed from red to yellow. In less than a minute it would change to green, meaning full power had been restored to all systems, including the elevator.

Ryan crept as close as he could get to the short alien, staying hidden behind any number of large pieces of equipment. Finally he arrived at yet another excavating vehicle about twenty yards away from his target. His heart was trying to pound its way out of his body but he couldn't get it to stop. He turned his body so the excavator, and Tezoc, were to his back, covered his ears and closed his eyes tightly.

"Now," he broadcast to his sister.

Regan threw her flashbang grenade and closed her eyes as well.

Her aim was perfect. The flashbang landed only a few feet from Carl and Tezoc and exploded instantly on impact. Battered by the shock wave from the explosion, Carl stumbled and went down, either dazed or unconscious. Tezoc managed to stay on his feet but was totally disoriented.

Ryan dashed out from behind the vehicle and sprinted toward Tezoc. When he was ten feet away from the alien he stopped, aimed the stun gun, and fired. Two electrode darts leapt out from the gun and stuck like

Velcro to Tezoc's black jumpsuit, discharging their electric payload in an instant. Tezoc's muscles convulsed, overwhelmed by the electricity, and he collapsed to the floor.

Regan joined her brother and pulled out a zip-strip. She bound the short alien's wrists behind him as they had done with Davidenko and Brice, and then rolled him onto his back. Ryan retracted the electrodes so the stun gun was ready to be fired again. Even though Tezoc was on the hard dirt floor of the cavern and bound, Ryan knelt on the ground and kept the gun firmly aimed at the alien's chest.

Carl was sprawled on the floor a few feet away, his eyes closed. He had a nasty gash on his cheek and he looked either dead or unconscious. Regan crawled to him to check for a pulse and was greatly relieved when she found one.

As usual, the effect of the flashbangs only lasted ten seconds or so and Tezoc had recovered, although he still wasn't fully recovered from the effects of the stun gun.

"How did you do it?" he bellowed. "It's not possible. How did you get through the barrier?" Then, after a moment of thought, he answered his own question. "You mean you actually *found* the force-field nullifier you were looking for," he said in disbelief. "The odds against that are one in a million."

"Sorry to disappoint you," replied Ryan.

Tezoc seethed, his hatred all-consuming. "I don't be-

193

lieve it!" he bellowed. "I should have killed you when I had the chance."

"If it makes you feel any better," noted Ryan, "your Captain Brice gave it his best shot."

"I underestimated you, after all. I knew you were talented, but I really never thought you could pose a threat all by yourselves."

"I guess you aren't as smart as you thought you were," said Regan.

"Maybe so," said Tezoc bitterly. "But you're forgetting one thing."

"What's that?" said Ryan.

Tezoc smiled. "You were correct in assuming it's more difficult for me to be active at the same time I control the mind of another. In fact, the way your minds are structured, a human couldn't do it at all. Like following two different movies on two screens at the same time. Your kind are completely incapable of it."

Ryan's forehead wrinkled in confusion. "So what's your point?"

"My point is this," replied Tezoc. "Humans can't do it." His eyes suddenly took on a maniacal gleam and he added chillingly, *But don't forget that I can!*

Ryan began to turn, panicked, as he finally realized the danger he was in, but it was too late. Although Carl was still on the cavern floor, his foot shot out and hit Ryan's arm with bone jarring force, sending Ryan's stun gun flying. Another savage kick sent Ryan reeling in the other direction, slamming into the ground and sliding about eight feet before finally coming to a rest, the breath knocked out of him.

Carl pulled out his pistol and fired at Ryan as he lay still on the ground. But just as he pulled the trigger Regan slammed into his arm as hard as she could, deflecting the shot just enough so that it missed her brother.

Carl knocked her to the floor effortlessly, as if she were made of straw. She slammed into the ground, stunned by the impact, and when she finally stopped skidding she was sprawled out awkwardly near Tezoc's head.

With both kids dazed and on the ground, Carl temporarily ignored them, sliding hurriedly to Tezoc. The alien rolled onto his stomach and Carl immediately went to work cutting through his restraints with a knife.

Complete and utter despair engulfed Regan like a dark storm cloud. They had come so close—only to fail in the end. Their situation had become hopeless. Carl was completely under Tezoc's control. Finding a way to defeat either one of them would have been hard enough, but defeating them both, now that the element of surprise was gone, was impossible. Tezoc was seconds away from being freed and once that happened the game was over. If only Carl . . .

Regan had a sudden flash of inspiration! Her eyes widened. Of course! She knew *exactly* what she needed to do.

One of her hands was sprawled out mere inches from Tezoc's head. She moved it slightly until she felt the bill of the alien's black baseball cap. In a single, smooth motion, she tore it off the alien's head and flung it like a Frisbee toward her brother. *"Grab the hat, Ryan!"* she screamed telepathically at the same instant. *"Do it!"*

Still stunned and fighting to regain his breath, Ryan rolled a foot or so to the hat and did what his sister had asked. He had no idea what she was doing but there was no time for questions. He grabbed the hat and realized as he did so that the hoop that went around the base of the cap was not elastic but was made from a hard, molded ceramic material. It was very similar to the superconducting material his dad had found, except it had an inner glow. It appeared to be somewhat fragile and had clearly been shaped and molded to perfectly fit Tezoc's head.

Carl had managed to free Tezoc at the same moment Regan had snatched the hat, flung it in her brother's direction, and issued her short telepathic order. The alien was still on his stomach as the last strand of his plasti-cuff restraint was severed.

Regan rolled as rapidly as she could past Tezoc's feet. Now free, the alien rolled onto his back and began to raise his gun to fire at Regan when he realized that the girl had come out of her roll with a stun gun pointed at his chest.

"Freeze!" shouted Regan at the top of her lungs.

Tezoc's eyes gleamed wildly. "You two are really getting on my nerves, you know that," he barked angrily. Then, forcing himself to calm down, he smiled and said, "It looks like we have a standoff, you and I. I think I'm faster than you but I still have some distance to go with the gun, so that makes us about even. In your game of chess, this is what is called a stalemate. A position from which neither one of us can win. So I'll make a deal with you. Lower that toy of yours and I'll let you and your brother live."

"Really," said Regan, unimpressed. "How generous of you." She raised her eyebrows. "Why don't you just have Colonel Sharp take it from me?"

Tezoc's face lit up with rage. Carl was just a few feet from him and straining with every muscle in his body to get at the short alien. He was being held back as if by an invisible hook, but the determination on his face was fierce and unmistakable.

"What's wrong, Tezoc? Having trouble controlling the colonel?" asked Regan innocently. "It sure looks that way. In fact, I'd say he looks like he wants to tear your head off with his bare hands."

The strain on Tezoc's face was growing by the second as they continued their standoff, his gun ready to move on Regan the instant she provided an opening.

"Here's what I think," said Regan. "I think your hat is more than just a fashion statement. You told us you invented an amplifier to boost your natural mental abilities. I'm guessing you would want a device like that as near to your brain as possible. If I were you," she continued knowingly, "I would put it in a hat."

Tezoc snarled fiercely. "And if I were *you*," he growled, "I would put down the stun gun. Because— clever as you are—I can outdraw you. And with my gun the damage will be permanent—and final."

"Think it through, Tezoc," challenged Regan. "You're so far away from your amplifier device that you can barely control the colonel. He's himself again. *And he doesn't look happy with you.* I can tell it's taking everything you've got just to stop him from crushing you into dust. But if you raise your gun even an inch to shoot me, my brother over there destroys your device instantly, and you lose your last shred of control over Colonel Sharp. Even if you were able to beat me to the trigger, you could never turn fast enough to stop the colonel. He would be on you in an instant."

Colonel Sharp continued his massive exertions to get at Tezoc, hatred and desire etched in every line of his face.

Regan had known that she couldn't defeat Tezoc and Carl both. She knew her only chance was to somehow free Carl of Tezoc's control, so he would be back on *their* side. In that instant the solution had clicked into place in her mind—and not a moment too soon.

"Turn and shoot my brother to save your device," continued Regan calmly, "and you could never turn back quickly enough to stop *me.*" She paused to let this sink in. "Turn to shoot Colonel Sharp and I'll stun you again before you can turn back."

A look of defeat came over the alien for the first time since he had arrived on Earth. The girl had him. There was no way out.

He lowered his gun in surrender. The moment he did so a loud crack reverberated throughout the cavern as Ryan snapped the cap's ceramic hoop in two.

The invisible force that held Carl back disappeared. Carl was Carl again and completely in control, and his fury was truly staggering. Tezoc had invaded his mind and caused him to do horrible acts against his will. He subdued Tezoc in an instant, having to use every ounce of his willpower to stop himself from tearing the alien apart.

Regan caught Tezoc's eye and shook her head. "Not stalemate, Tezoc," she said defiantly. *"Checkmate."*

CHAPTER 25

Reactivation

With the help once again of Regan's force-field nullifier, they entered the city. Carl marched the prisoner to his headquarters building nearby, eager to have access to the computer and communications systems there. During the short trip the siblings hurriedly filled him in on recent events. He had been bound and unconscious in the back of a Hauler and knew nothing of the conversations that had taken place at the site at which Ben Resnick was attempting to create an exit. Even if he had been awake and next to the real Tezoc at the time, he wouldn't have heard anything since Tezoc's words were coming from the mouth of his puppet, Lieutenant Adams, several miles distant.

When they arrived at security headquarters Carl didn't take any chances with the prisoner, binding him so tightly and in so many ways that escape was impossible. He quickly restarted all electronic security systems in Prometheus and the outer perimeter. He then activated all security personnel who hadn't been captured by Tezoc, invoking the highest emergency priority level that existed.

This came as quite a surprise to them, to say the least. Ten minutes earlier he had called and told them the lock-down was proceeding smoothly and they could take additional time off. He had said he was about to step into the elevator for his meeting with the Secret Service and didn't want to be disturbed. Carl's men weren't quite sure what game he was playing, but he had used all the proper codes both times.

Carl ordered most of his remaining security team to double-time it into the cavern where he would meet them. Some would be dispatched to quickly remove the mercenaries from the city before they awoke. Others would look after the members of the Prometheus Project as they regained consciousness. Ryan and Regan waited patiently beside him as he activated systems and dispatched orders.

With this taken care of, Carl bandaged up the gash in his cheek, which was still bleeding, and turned to the two siblings. Both now had numerous cuts and bruises, and their clothing was dirty and tattered. He inspected them carefully and made sure none of their injuries were serious.

"Look . . . kids," he said, horror etched in every line

of his face. "I am so sorry. I almost killed you. I don't know what to say."

"You don't have to say anything," responded Ryan immediately. "It was Tezoc who tried to kill us. We know that wasn't really you, and there was nothing you could do about it. We know the *real* you would never hurt us in a million years."

Regan nodded her agreement beside him. She smiled. "I'm just glad you're our friend and not our enemy." She gently touched her bruised arm and winced. "You're even stronger than I thought."

Carl placed a large hand on each of their shoulders and met their eyes with affection and a deeply felt respect. "Kids, there is no way I'll ever be able to thank you enough. You saved me from this madman. You saved us all."

Both kids beamed happily. "Thanks," said Ryan sheepishly, a little embarrassed to receive such lavish praise. "But we did have a great teacher. Not every kid gets to learn about military weaponry and strategy from the famous Colonel Carl Sharp."

Carl laughed. "Yeah. It's nice to know you guys were paying attention. No one has ever used a flashbang grenade or a stun gun any better," he said. "And it's nice of you to give me some credit, but I'm not going for it. This is definitely a case in which the students have outdone the teacher. If I were as clever as either of you I'd be the famous General Carl Sharp. Heck, I'd be the famous *Chairman of the Joint Chiefs of Staff* Carl Sharp." Carl lowered his eyes and shook his head miserably. "It's my job to protect this place—and you. And I failed. I let myself get caught off-guard and be rendered helpless. I wasn't able to find a single way to help you."

"You're being too hard on yourself. You didn't fail," insisted Regan. "And Tezoc didn't catch you off guard. He used his amplified mental abilities to knock you out. There's no defense against that."

"She's absolutely right," echoed Ryan.

Carl sighed unhappily. "I suppose so," he muttered, but the frown did not leave his face and he was clearly not convinced.

"What was it like, anyway?" said Ryan. "You know, to have Tezoc . . . well, you don't have to answer this if you'd rather not, but to be . . . to be—"

"Controlled by him," finished Carl.

Ryan nodded grimly.

"It was the most horrible experience I've ever had," said Carl, shuddering at the memory. "I tried to fight him, to push him from my mind, but my efforts were totally useless. All I could do was watch helplessly as he raided my mind for information and used my body as if it were his own. And while he was in my mind, I got a glimpse into his as well. That might have been the worst part. His mind was so diseased, so poisonous.

There was such evil there; such hatred and cruelty." He shook his head solemnly. "It was a waking nightmare, and there was nothing I could do about it."

"How awful," said Regan, appalled. She paused. "Do you remember any of the other times he controlled you or just this latest one?"

"Only this one. I saw in his mind that he had controlled me before, while breaking out of the city and back into it, but I had no memory of these events. While he was in my mind, just before he exited each time, he must have been able to find and eliminate those memories."

Ryan opened his mouth to ask another question but Carl raised a hand to cut him off. "Sorry," said Carl, glancing at this watch. "But we'll have to finish this conversation later. I have to meet my men in the cavern so I can let them into the city with the nullifier, and I still have a few things I need to do." He motioned to his cushioned chairs. "Go ahead and make yourselves comfortable and I'll be with you in about ten minutes or so."

Carl spent almost five minutes making sure all systems were fully back on line while Ryan and his sister talked, and planned, in private. Finally, he called the Secret Service to let them know he needed to postpone the president's visit to run down a possible problem. He was in no mood to go into details and he knew he would be up all hours of the night preparing a full report in any case.

While Carl was on the phone with the Secret Service, Ryan and Regan approached the prisoner. He was tightly bound to a chair. Thin steel cable was wrapped several times around him and the chair, and loops on each end of the cable were padlocked together. His hands were bound up tightly behind his back with heavy tape, several zip-strips, and metal handcuffs, and his ankles had received the same treatment.

Tezoc glared at them hatefully. "Leave me alone," he growled.

"Okay," said Ryan. "No problem. But first, we need you to reactivate the city's central computer."

Tezoc laughed. "You have to be kidding. You've just ruined a plan that has taken me seven years working day and night to perfect. What could possibly make you think I would *ever* do anything for you?" he spat.

They had fully expected this response and had planned for it. "Oh, we aren't asking you to do it for *us*," said Regan innocently. "We want you to do it for yourself, Tezoc. If you activate the central computer, we promise to try to convince it to send you back to your own world for justice. We can't be sure it will listen to us, but it has before."

Tezoc glared but said nothing.

"On the other hand," continued Ryan. "If you don't, I know Colonel Sharp will look forward to making sure you're punished for your crimes here on Earth. The colonel is an extremely fair man. But when someone invades his mind and body and tries to kill everyone he cares about and take over his planet, *he loses his sense of humor.* I don't think you'll enjoy your stay on Earth from now on. You said the prisons on Morca were like luxury resorts. Trust me, you'll never confuse the tiny, isolated, windowless, concrete cell that Colonel Sharp throws you into for a luxury resort. That is, if you're lucky enough to even get a cell *that* nice."

"Then again," added Regan, "since you're the only intelligent alien on Earth, biologists will be eager to study you. I'm sure that a few hours each day of having every last inch of your body examined by teams of doctors will at least give you a break from your cold, damp prison cell."

"Of course you've proven your ability to escape prisons," said Ryan. "So it's possible the authorities will decide you're far too dangerous to be kept alive, no matter how good the prison. I don't think that will happen, but you never know."

Ryan paused to let his words sink in. "Think it over," he finished evenly.

Tezoc said nothing for a long while, just continuing to glare at them icily. Finally he spoke. "I would not have believed it possible," he said in clipped tones, barely controlling his rage. "But I truly believe I'm coming to despise the two of you more than I despise the Qwervy."

Regan smiled. "Thanks," she said. "We're honored."

Tezoc knew he was beaten. Still scowling, he tilted his head, and they felt his mental energy brush against them as he broadcast reactivation codes.

Almost instantly the Teacher was back!

They could both feel the slight glow in their minds that indicated its presence.

"Children," it said telepathically by way of greeting. *"Would it be okay if I entered your minds to learn what is happening?"*

They both agreed immediately. The Teacher entered their minds in super-accelerated mode and in less than a second was able to relive their every experience since it had been shut down.

"Kids," it broadcast telepathically. *"I can't thank you enough for what you have done."* It paused for several seconds. *"I have just been in contact with the Qwervy,"* it broadcast, *"in accelerated mode. I have relayed all that has happened here. You have impressed the Qwervy greatly. And please believe me when I tell you that they don't impress easily."*

"Does this mean you'll be able to communicate with us from now on?" asked Regan eagerly.

"I'm afraid not," replied the teacher in disappointment. *"After this brief conversation I will still be unable to communicate with you or help your team in any way. You know I have become very fond of you both, and you are both quite deserving. But the Qwervy still need to see if humanity can be mature with your use of*

the technology in this city, without any help or interfer-
ence. And speaking of interference, the Qwervy express
their deepest apologies that you were forced to suffer
Tezoc's interference in your affairs. Let me assure you
they won't let this happen again."

The Teacher paused. *"Regarding Tezoc, the Qwervy*
agree that he should be sent to Morca for punishment.
Not because Earth doesn't have the greatest claim to
hold him for his crimes against you, but because the
Qwervy are worried for your safety. This prisoner is too
dangerous and too resourceful. If he were to escape on
Earth the consequences would be catastrophic. But rest
assured, the Qwervy will take a role in ensuring he re-
ceives the punishment he deserves and that he can never
escape again.

"In a moment I will contact Colonel Sharp telepath-
ically. I will keep my identity as the city's central com-
puter a secret. I will tell him I am contacting him from
the Morcan home world and explain my wishes that the
prisoner be turned over to us. I will also explain to him
why. Then I will instruct him to send Tezoc through a
portal in the zoo. I will reprogram it so the portal takes
him directly to the Morcan authorities."

"Before you do, can you stay and talk for a while?"
asked Ryan.

"You don't know how sorry I am, but I cannot."
It was easy for the siblings to pick up the deep over-
tones of disappointment in the Teacher's telepathic com-

munication. *"Goodbye kids. I will take my leave now. But before I do, I have one last thing I would like to transmit."*

The Teacher paused. *"Well done,"* it broadcast warmly. *"Very well done."*

CHAPTER 26

An Important Visitor

The rest of the weekend had been a whirlwind. The members of the Prometheus team had finally awakened within the city on Saturday after sleeping for hours. The mercs had been removed from Prometheus and transported separately to other locations so they wouldn't wake up in, or near, the alien city, and they couldn't compare notes.

The memory erasing inhalant that Carl's Proact scientists had developed worked beautifully, and the mercs had no memories of their experiences within Prometheus. It wasn't difficult on an individual basis to convince them they had gone temporarily insane the week before; imagining being contacted by a man of towering height, who claimed to be an alien, ranting and raving about a huge alien city a mile beneath the ground. And while it wasn't fair to charge them with invading Prometheus since they had been under Tezoc's influence at the time, they were all wanted for other crimes—especially Brice.

Carl explained to Dr. Harris and the team that the Morcans had contacted him telepathically and had recommended, for Earth's safety, that Tezoc be transferred into their custody as quickly as possible. The team unanimously agreed and sent Tezoc through a portal to the Morcan home world within hours of the team's awakening. To say that everyone was thrilled and greatly relieved to be rid of the ruthless alien was an understatement.

On Sunday the entire Prometheus team and every member of security not on duty gathered together while Ryan and Regan reviewed everything that had happened and answered questions. They were showered with so much praise and gratitude they began to feel awkward, but there was a part of both of them that enjoyed every second of it.

Finally, the longest weekend of their lives ended late Sunday night, and they were asleep before their heads hit their pillows.

When they awoke Monday morning, their parents insisted that they take it easy and not rush to school. They would have a big family breakfast and if they were late to school by an hour or so, so be it.

The entire family was in good spirits as they sat around their rectangular, oak kitchen table for breakfast, looking out of their large picture window at the thick woods just beyond their backyard.

"We're giving you an extra hour to get to school, but are you two even sure you're ready to go back at all today after everything that happened this weekend?" asked Mrs. Resnick.

Ryan nodded. "*Definitely.* I'm looking forward to seeing my friends and spending a normal day in class. I've had enough adventure for a while."

"You can say that again," agreed Regan.

"Well, you two have become quite the celebrities on the team," said Mr. Resnick. "I just hope you don't let it go to your head."

Ryan's eyes twinkled playfully. "Well *I* won't, Dad, but I don't know about Regan. All I did was help save the world. But by finding a nullifier Regan did something really impressive: she proved you wrong about something having to do with science."

Ben Resnick laughed heartily. "I wish proving me wrong was really that special, Ryan," he said modestly. "But I must admit that in this case it was impressive, indeed. I couldn't be prouder, as I've already made it very clear to her. And you, Ryan, what can I say: even when you were a little boy you had a talent for smashing things to bits with a hammer. Nice work."

Ryan laughed.

"Just to get serious for a second," said Regan, "with school and all, we really don't have as much chance to explore the city as we want. And it takes forever to get through security. I'm starting to think we should do this sleepover thing more often. Maybe once a month or so on a Friday or Saturday night."

Amanda Resnick almost choked on a mouthful of scrambled eggs. "What? After what just happened? You have to be kidding."

"Okay, Mom," said Regan. "I'll admit the sleepover turned out to be just slightly more dangerous than we had thought, but there's no way something like that could ever happen again."

"Just *slightly* more dangerous?" said her mom in disbelief. "That's like saying the Earth is just *slightly* bigger than an ant."

Ben Resnick raised his eyebrows. "On the other hand, Amanda, if we hadn't let them have their sleepover, everyone who was in the city would be dead and Tezoc would be taking over the planet right now."

"Good point, Dad," said Ryan. "See, Mom. You made a great decision letting us stay. Heck, you could win that mother-of-the-year award, after all."

Amanda Resnick smiled and rolled her eyes. She was about to respond when the doorbell rang.

That was odd, thought Regan. There were few people living nearby and they rarely got visitors. But their mother didn't seem to be surprised at all.

"We'll have to discuss this sleepover business another time," said Mrs. Resnick, rising to get the door. She motioned for her children to follow her. She reached the door and threw it open.

Three men stood at the doorway. Two of them were Colonel Carl Sharp, in full dress uniform, and Dr. Harry Harris.

The other was the President of the United States.

Kevin Quinn. *President* Kevin Quinn. Looking quite comfortable in his loose-fitting gray suit and blue necktie.

Regan shook her head as if to clear a dream. No, that didn't work. He was still there. *The president.* He looked taller and thinner than he did on TV, but there could be no doubt that it was he. He was a trim, handsome man of fifty-five with a strong chin and dark hair peppered with gray.

About thirty yards behind the president, parked beside a massive tree near the gravel road to their house, were two stretch limousines with dark, bulletproof windows. Six Secret Service agents wearing dark suits and extremely serious expressions had taken up positions around their yard, watching for any possible trouble while they waited for the president to complete his business.

"Hello Ben . . . Amanda," said President Quinn, shaking their hands, his voice deep and commanding.

"Mom and Dad know the president!" broadcast Ryan in disbelief.

"It sure looks that way," replied Regan.

"Come in, come in," said Ben Resnick.

The three men entered and Mrs. Resnick closed the door behind them.

Ben Resnick faced Kevin Quinn. "I'm glad you could make it, Mr. President."

"Me too," said the president sincerely. "But, unfortunately, I only have a few minutes. I've been at Prometheus since dawn and I need to get back there and complete my visit." He grinned good-naturedly. "You may have heard that my planned visit on Saturday had to be rescheduled. Seems I was about to walk into an ambush."

"I did hear something about that," said their father, trying to keep a straight face and failing.

"But I was determined to fit this in, no matter how much juggling of my schedule I had to do. Sorry about making the kids late for school."

Amanda Resnick smiled. "That's quite all right. I'm sure they'll catch up."

He turned toward the kids. "As you have no doubt figured out by now, I have come here this morning to meet the youngest members of the Prometheus team. I had your parents hold you up from school so you'd still be here," he explained. "I'm here to thank you personally for everything you've done." He shook hands warmly with each of the Resnick kids in turn. "Ryan . . . Regan," he said, "I have read the colonel's report, and I have to say we're all extremely lucky you're on the team.

215

You know, when Dr. Harris told me he was adding two children to his team, I really thought he was crazy. Not anymore," he said simply. *"Definitely* not anymore."

"Thanks, ah . . . sir," said Ryan, and his sister added her thanks as well.

"Don't thank me," he said. "I'm here to thank you. Not only have your actions saved the city itself and the lives of the people who were inside of it on Saturday, but you have also saved many billions of others from a truly horrible future at the mercy of a ruthless tyrant. So on behalf of the United States and the peoples of the world, please accept my sincere thanks. We are all in your debt."

They both nodded as if in a trance, too stunned and overwhelmed to speak.

"Unfortunately, my thanks and deep appreciation are all I can offer you—for now at least. Have you ever heard of something called the Presidential Medal of Freedom?"

They both shook their heads no, still mesmerized by the president's praise and his rich, deep voice.

"It's the single highest civilian award in the United States, given to recognize individuals who have made a major contribution to the security or national interests of our country. Recipients are determined by the president alone." He smiled and nodded warmly at the siblings. "I'm happy to say that your actions in stopping the threat posed by this hostile alien, this um . . . Tezoc . . .

more than qualify you for this honor, and I have made the decision to award this medal to each of you." Before they could get too excited, frowning deeply, he hurriedly added, "But there is a catch."

President Quinn paused. Everyone in the room waited anxiously for him to continue, wondering where he was headed.

"Here's the problem," said the president in frustration. "The Prometheus Project, and your involvement with it, could not have a higher top-secret classification. The purpose of the Presidential Medal of Freedom is to recognize outstanding accomplishment—publicly. So the country and the world can know what you have done. The only way I could give you what you've earned would be in total secret, which would defeat the purpose of the honor." He paused. "So while I've signed a secret order giving you this award, the ceremony and presentation of the medals will be postponed until such time as this project is declassified, even if I'm no longer in office at the time. While I can't tell you how much I wish I could just invite you to the White House tomorrow for a public ceremony, that isn't possible. But know this: the medals will always be waiting for you, no matter how long it takes. I am truly sorry about this."

Both kids' mouths hung open in astonishment and delight.

"Sorry?" said Ryan in disbelief. "There is no need to be sorry . . . ah, sir," he added happily. "Thanks. Thanks a lot. It's a fantastic honor. We don't have to have the medals in our hands to appreciate it."

Regan nodded her agreement. "Right. We understand why you can't give them out now, sir. Just knowing that you wanted to do this, all by itself, is incredible."

The president tilted his head slightly and grinned. "You two really are something," he noted, impressed by their reaction. "Well, congratulations. You should know that you are, *by far*, the youngest recipients of this medal ever." He raised his eyebrows. "Although I must admit that it's possible you'll be my age before you finally receive them."

President Quinn sighed. "Unfortunately, I have to go now. But you both are quite remarkable, and I'd really like to spend some more time getting to know you better during my next visit to Prometheus."

"We would be honored, Mr. President," said Regan.

"Yes, anytime you would like, sir," added Ryan.

The president nodded. "I'll look forward to it."

Dr. Harris and Carl said their goodbyes as well and headed for the door. Just as they reached it the president turned and scratched his head. "Ben, Amanda," he said. "Have you ever considered having more children?"

"Ah . . . no, Mr. President," replied Ben Resnick, having been caught completely off-guard by the question. "Ah . . . not for a while now, sir."

"Well, maybe you should," said the president playfully. "Consider doing it for your country. As your patriotic duty. We could really use five or ten more kids like these two."

Amanda Resnick's eyes went wide. "Five or ten, sir?" she said, pretending to be alarmed.

"Well, ten or twenty would be better," said the president, a huge smile coming over his handsome features. "But you're obviously a very busy woman, so I would never ask you to have more than ten."

"Thank you, Mr. President," replied Amanda Resnick, fighting to keep a straight face. "That's very reasonable of you, sir," she added.

CHAPTER 27

Underachievers

Ryan and Regan Resnick were signing in at the front office of their school when the principal, Lynda Lyons, poked her nose out of her office door. She saw the two siblings and shook her head. Five or ten minutes was one thing, but this time they were over an *hour* late. And they didn't look guilty about it either. In fact, they looked so happy they were almost glowing.

There was something not quite right about these two kids. They were well behaved and did well enough at school, but they never seemed to go the extra mile. They were classic underachievers. They never did any extra-credit work. Neither one had even taken part in a recent Science Fair competition.

She had read in their files that their parents were both accomplished scientists and had even heard from their teachers that they wanted to be scientists when they grew up. Well, they would never become great scientists if they never made any effort to learn about science outside of the classroom, that was for sure. And if this wasn't troubling enough, they both seemed to be the last students to get to school in the morning and often the first two to race out the door.

But race to where? They were involved in precious few extracurricular activities. This was Brewster Pennsylvania, after all, and there just wasn't that much to do. Because of this, participation in extracurricular activities was very high. There were so many activities to choose from it was hard to imagine a student not being able to find several they enjoyed. And the alternative around here was most often boredom, since there wasn't even a movie theater or any other sign of civilization within a hundred miles of the town.

She stepped from her office. "Hello, Ryan," she said. "Hello, Regan."

"Hello Principal Lyons," they both replied cheerfully.

"Running a little late, are we?"

"Sorry. We'll try to work on that," promised Regan.

"Forget to set the alarm this morning?"

Ryan eyed his sister mischievously. "I don't suppose you'd believe that we were meeting with President Quinn because he wanted to thank us personally for everything we've done."

Principal Lyons looked at them crossly. "No, Ryan, I don't suppose I would."

Ryan managed not to grin but he couldn't help wearing an amused look on his face. "I didn't think so," he said. "Okay, in that case, we overslept."

"Overslept," repeated Principal Lyons knowingly. "Just as I thought. From everything I hear, you two are great kids. I just wish you'd put in some more effort. I really think the two of you are capable of extraordinary achievements if you would just apply yourselves."

"You really think so?" said Regan.

"I really do," said the principal. "I know you aren't involved in many extracurricular activities. What do you find to do with yourselves? This is a pretty isolated part of the world."

"We keep busy," said Ryan.

"Well, what did you do this weekend for example? I don't want to pry, so only tell me what you're comfortable telling me, but did you do anything productive? Anything exciting? Anything challenging?"

"I'm gonna say, yes," said Regan.

"Definitely yes," agreed Ryan.

"Like what?" pressed the principal.

"*Uh-oh,*" broadcast Ryan. "*Any ideas?*"

"*None,*" replied Regan. "*Maybe we should just surrender.*"

Ryan sighed heavily. "Okay, Principal Lyons, I'm gonna level with you. Regan and I don't need much excitement. We just like hanging out at our house, spending time with friends, reading a little, doing a little hiking. I know a lot of kids our age need to be doing something exciting all the time, but not us."

The principal nodded. "And there is nothing wrong with that," she said. "Nothing at all. I just want to make sure you two live up to your potential. I would love for you to find something you could get excited about. To find something challenging to pursue that really interests you."

"We appreciate the advice," said Regan.

"Yeah. We'll keep our eyes open," promised Ryan. "Who knows? Maybe we'll stumble onto something like that, after all."

"Right," agreed Regan. "You never know. It could happen." She glanced at her brother and smiled. "To be honest with you, since we arrived in Brewster," she continued with a twinkle in her eye, "I've begun to believe that just about anything is possible."

The Adventure Continues...

The Prometheus Project
Book 3
Stranded

Ryan and Regan Resnick are trapped on a treacherous alien planet, surrounded by vicious predators, and in the path of a raging river of lava. And their troubles are only beginning . . .

When the Resnick kids become stranded on a primitive planet, they are plunged into a nonstop fight for their lives. But surviving on the deadly planet might be the *easy* part. Because if they can get back to Earth, they will have to face a ruthless adversary who controls a mysterious alien device. A device that is the most powerful, dangerous, and unstoppable weapon the world has ever known . . .

Bonus Chapter

Why Did Tezoc Zoron First
Set His Sights on Earth?

How Was he Able to Plan For This
Conquest While in Prison?

Turn The Page to Read a Bonus Chapter
That Answers These Questions.

The Alien Prisoner

This chapter was the first ever written for CAPTURED. It was written from Tezoc Zoron's point of view, and was the beginning chapter of the very first draft of the book (although it didn't make it into the final version). It takes place seven years before the events chronicled in CAPTURED.

Tezoc Zoron surveyed the prison's vast grounds and lavish facilities from inside the enormous mansion that served as his private prison cell. He sneered bitterly.

Sheep, he thought in disgust. The people of the planet Morca had become nothing more than pathetic sheep. He was sickened to be a member of the species.

He had committed unspeakable crimes, and how had they chosen to punish him?—by placing him in a prison that was grander than a palace. He shook his head. The Morcans had become so soft that comparing them to sheep was an insult to the *sheep.*

He walked to his study and sat in a recliner that instantly counterbalanced his weight, even as he shifted, exactly mimicking the effects of total weightlessness.

But as much as he despised his own people, he hated an arrogant alien species called the Qwervy even more. He had just entered prison five years earlier when they had revealed themselves to the Morcans. The Qwervy were the species at the top of the food chain in a galactic collection of civilizations linked together by a vast web of portals. Step through a portal and you were on another world, even if it was trillions of miles away.

Prior to this time the Morcans had been completely unaware of this galactic community. But that didn't mean the galactic community was unaware of Morca.

Oh no, quite the opposite.

It turned out that the Qwervy had established an underground city from which they had secretly observed the Morcans for hundreds of years. During this time, the Morcans were apparently not advanced enough, not *mature* enough, to join this galactic community. Until now. How lucky for the Morcans that the Qwervy had finally found them worthy to sit at the grown-up table.

It was an outrage! The Morcans had been spied upon and treated like children. Who were the Qwervy to sit in judgment of them? Who were the Qwervy to snub Morca as they had for hundreds of years? Yes, the Qwervy had superior technology, but only because they were the *oldest* species in the galaxy, not because *they* were superior.

And just like sheep, the Morcan's couldn't wait to flock to this galactic society, to abandon their old way of life to cavort with *aliens*—aliens who must surely be laughing in secret at the pathetic newcomers to their galactic club.

Well Tezoc wasn't a sheep. Fire and pride still burned

in his veins. He was unique—and everyone knew it. He was widely regarded as the most brilliant and most dangerous Morcan on the planet.

And the greatest insult of all—the Qwervy had contacted him in prison and offered to cure him of what they called his mental illness, eliminating his ruthless and unstable behavior. Cure *him?* It was the rest of his people that needed curing, not him. Would a powerful, cunning, perfectly adapted carnivore agree to be turned into a tame, spineless grass-eater? No, of course not. And neither would Tezoc.

He directed a thought at the wall and a glass emerged, instantly filled with his favorite drink. Invisible tractor beams of energy shuttled it quickly to his hand.

But as weak and pathetic as his fellow Morcans were, they had—finally—managed to capture him, and if he escaped they would do so yet again. They had recorded his brain wave patterns, something impossible for him to disguise, and had technology that would allow them to track him down, wherever he went. At least wherever he went on the planet Morca.

But because of the Qwervy he could now leave Morca altogether. As much as he loathed them, they had done him an enormous favor. He could use their portals to travel to another planet to amass immense power, right under their noses. And while this would be exceptionally difficult, he was as patient as he was brilliant—and he had all the time in the world to plan. He might be a prisoner, but he still had access to Morca's extraordinarily advanced central computer.

"Computer," he said after having accessed it, "I want to ask you some questions. Will this conversation be absolutely private?"

"Yes. Even though you are a criminal and a prisoner, you have the right to privacy . . . with one exception."

"Which is?"

"I am not authorized to provide you with any information on prison security or any technology being used to keep you a prisoner here. If you ask me for any information that might help you escape, I will not answer and I will be forced to alert the authorities. Otherwise, our conversation will be private and I will provide you with any assistance I can."

Tezoc nodded thoughtfully. "How about when we're finished. Can I order you to erase all evidence our conversation ever took place?"

"No. You cannot. Our discussion will be recorded permanently and cannot be deleted. I can, however, seal the conversation so that only you can access it."

Tezoc took a long sip of his drink and let go of his glass. The tractor beams caught it instantly and it hovered before him as he continued. "Suppose you sealed our conversation and—speaking totally hypothetically, of course—I were to escape," he said calmly. "Would this be grounds for the authorities to break the seal?"

"No one has ever escaped from a modern Morcan prison," pointed out the computer.

The corners of Tezoc's mouth turned upward in a slight smile. "Of course, of course. Since escape is impossible and I have no interest in escaping in any event, I only ask out of idle curiosity."

"The conversation would be sealed no matter what, even if you were to escape and even if you were to commit further criminal acts. No one but you could ever retrieve it."

Tezoc nodded, satisfied. It was very thoughtful of the sheep to protect the privacy rights of the carnivores. "Then do so. Seal this conversation and all other conversations and interactions between us until I tell you otherwise."

"Acknowledged."

"Okay, let us begin. How many planets are connected together by portals?"

"This number is growing so rapidly that by the time I communicate the precise number to you it will have changed."

"*Approximately* how many?" snapped Tezoc impatiently.

"Nine million."

Tezoc whistled. The Qwervy and their community of alien species had been busy.

"How many of these planets are members of the galactic community?"

"As of today, 397."

"Just 397? Out of nine million? What about the rest of them?"

"Other than these 397, almost all of the rest are primitive, devoid of intelligent life or civilizations. These can be accessed freely by all members of the galactic community."

"You said *almost* all of the rest are primitive. Which means there must be yet another category."

"Yes. This category is comprised of worlds containing civilizations that have not advanced enough for membership in the galactic community. Each of these is under periodic observation by the Qwervy or other member species. These worlds are restricted. Only a few authorized observers are allowed to visit."

Tezoc nodded. "How many, exactly, are in this category?"

"As of today, 268."

Tezoc paused in thought. "And how many of these have achieved a technology advanced enough to harness nuclear power and to have simple computers?"

"One hundred and forty-seven."

"Of these, on how many could a Morcan disguise himself as a member of the dominant, intelligent species without major surgery? Don't worry about differences in internal organs and the like, just outward appearance."

"Working . . . thirty-eight. In some of these cases, the disguise would only require a few changes that could be done with simple makeup. In others, the disguise would require sophisticated masks of the type produced by special effects experts who work on actors."

This had been a difficult question. It had taken the computer almost a second to answer.

"Computer, I have saved a file on my compu-pad entitled, *desired mental frequencies*. Please upload this file."

"Working . . . uploaded and read."

"Good. How many of these thirty-eight species have brain architecture that fits the profile listed in this file?"

"Three."

"Do the Qwervy consider all three of these species to be equally promising?"

"No. Surprisingly enough, one of the three is considered to be more promising than any of the other 268 known pre-galactic species. So promising, in fact, they are even thought to have the potential to surpass all of the advanced species in the galactic community some- day, including the Qwervy. They are a very young species in galactic terms, but they are advancing at a rate never before seen. Unfortunately, they are also thought to have the potential to become one of the most dangerous spe- cies ever known."

Tezoc smiled for the first time. Perfect. They were just like him—brilliant but dangerous. Who wanted to rule a race of sheep, after all.

"And the location of the planet on which this species lives?"

"Like Morca, it is in the Milky Way galaxy. It is 26,000 light-years from the center of the galaxy, on the edge of one of its four spiral arms, and 8,000 light-years away from Morca."

Tezoc nodded. This was an incomprehensible dis- tance, but it meant nothing now. Thanks to the almighty Qwervy, the planet was just a portal step away.

"And the name of this planet?"

"The inhabitants call it simply, *Earth*."

Tezoc repeated the word slowly, letting it roll off his tongue. "Eeeartth." His eyes brightened as his hatred of the Qwervy was momentarily forgotten. "Okay, down- load all information you have on the planet Earth into my compu-pad."

"Working . . . download completed."

"Project a hologram of the planet," ordered Tezoc.

"Acknowledged," replied the computer as a blue- green globe suddenly appeared in front of Tezoc and his floating drink. The globe began slowly revolving.

"Good. I want to remind you that I'm asking nothing about escaping from this prison, nor will I ever." He paused. "With that understood, please download all information you have regarding the workings of the portals into my compu-pad."

"The file is enormous and will leave you with almost no memory in your compu-pad."

"Understood. Do it anyway."

"Working . . . download completed."

"Good. Do you know the security measures that prevent unauthorized persons from traveling to these restricted planets?"

"Yes."

"Do you know how to bypass this security?"

"No."

Tezoc nodded, not at all surprised. "Okay, here is what you and I are going to do. Together, we're going to figure out a way that a man could bypass Qwervy portal security—again, not prison security, but portal security—and travel to this planet *Earth*. We are then going to find a way that this same man could erase all evidence of this trip and close the portal down behind him, ensuring that no one knows where he is or can follow him."

"For what purpose?"

"Since it doesn't involve escape from this prison," replied Tezoc smoothly, "this is none of your concern. However, since we're going to be partners for many years, I will tell you. I need to work on something that will stimulate my mind while I'm in prison. I've chosen this problem because it's interesting and challenging, and for no other reason."

"You are certain this is a good idea? It is not clear that

this problem can be solved. Even if it can be, finding a solution will almost certainly take many years of constant effort."

Tezoc smiled and spread his arms to take in the spacious prison surrounding him. "I'm not going anywhere for a long, long time. This is the perfect challenge."

The computer wasn't entirely satisfied. "My second concern is for your mental health. Even if we find a way to defeat portal security to travel to Earth, if you believe you will somehow be able to escape this prison to carry out this plan, you will be very disappointed. You cannot escape from this prison."

"Of course not," replied Tezoc, an amused tone in his voice. "Escape is impossible. Everyone knows that."

"Good," replied the computer. "I would not want you to suffer such great disappointment."

Tezoc smiled without humor. "Don't you worry about me," he said coolly as a fierce gleam came to his eye. "The last thing I plan to be is disappointed."

Tezoc paused for a long moment deep in thought. "One last thing," he said finally. "I have an idea for an invention. For a device I can use to amplify and enhance certain of my mental capabilities. Will you provide me with the parts and supplies I need to build it?"

"Provided these parts cannot be used in an attempted escape," replied the computer predictably, "and provided I analyze and approve the plans. As long as the invention cannot be used to harm anyone on Morca, I will approve it."

"Good," said Tezoc coolly. "Very good." His eyes locked firmly on the blue-green globe floating before him. "Then there is nothing to worry about. As you will soon see, my invention cannot be used to harm anyone." He watched the small globe complete yet another of its slow revolutions and the corners of his mouth turned up in a cruel, satisfied smile.

"At least not anyone on Morca," he finished icily.

About The Author

DOUGLAS E. RICHARDS is a former biotechnology executive who has written extensively for the award-winning magazine, *National Geographic KIDS,* and also for *American Fencing Magazine.* He currently lives in San Diego, California with his wife, Kelly, his children, Ryan and Regan (for whom the main characters in his Prometheus Project series are named), and his dog Dash. After graduating with a BS in microbiology from the Ohio State University, he earned a master's degree in molecular biology from the University of Wisconsin and a master's in business administration from the University of Chicago. To learn more about Douglas and his work, please visit *www.douglaserichards.com.*

About the Author

DOUGLAS E. RICHARDS ...